For Na

The Lost Pearl

lara zuberi

Hope you enjoy it!

Lara
3/10/13

Author's Note: All characters are fictitious and any resemblance to any person is purely coincidental. The brief discussions regarding events in recent history are simply meant to provide a backdrop for the novel. The translations of excerpts of poetry by Faiz Ahmed Faiz and Parveen Shakir are not claimed to be exact or authentic, but rather are the author's own attempt at conveying a small fraction of what was expressed by their timeless words.

ISBN: 1-4774-5374-1
ISBN-13: 9781477453742

Dedication

To Mummy and Daddy, for inspiring the opening line of this book;

My husband, Omer, for his unwavering support; and

My son, Aariz, for being the sunshine that illuminates every day of my life.

Chapter 1

It was the perfect childhood—that is until everything changed, of course. It was February 1987, and we were enjoying another mild Karachi winter. We had lived in the same house in Pakistan since my birth, and the most recent addition to it was our family portrait, which had acquired the status of becoming the most outstanding feature of my father's study. Surrounded by an intricate bronze frame, it had originally been placed in the family room, but Papa insisted on moving it, arguing that he spent a greater fraction of his time at his desk and wanted our picture to be simply a glance away. He had retrieved his hammer and nails from his old toolbox and fixed the portrait to the wall across from his desk despite my mother's insistence that it remain in the family room. He asked me to confirm that it was centered and straight before finalizing its position on the wall.

It was a lovely photograph taken six months earlier, with my father a handsome man of forty, his wavy hair gelled back, revealing some subtle streaks of gray. He was wearing his thick black glasses, which in my humble opinion were too old-fashioned and in need of replacement by thinner metallic ones. He was dressed in his usual collared shirt, bleached to the brightest shade of white. He wore a diagonally striped blue-and-black silk tie that gave him the look of a truly distinguished gentleman, the silver links of his watch barely emerging from the edge of his starched sleeve. Next to him was my beautiful mother, six months shy of her thirtieth birthday, the epitome of poise and elegance, adorned in a traditional Pakistani dress, a pink *kurta shalwar* with a delicately embroidered design. Her face beamed with joy, and her stunning eyes shone with pride, a reflection of everything having gone well in her life, perhaps. In her lap was my four-year-old brother, Sahir, dressed in a very proper dark red shirt, mischief unable to escape his chubby face. His straight black hair fell generously on his forehead, nearly covering his eyes. It had taken countless attempts to make him stationary for the pose, superseding the difficulty with which he had agreed to be still for his haircut a month before.

In the center was me, a nine-year-old girl with long black hair brushed neatly into two braids and tied with bright yellow ribbons on either side of a very straight middle parting. They matched the yellow-and-white summer dress I was wearing, which my aunt had thoughtfully sent as a birthday present. Anyone who saw the photograph would be compelled to notice the striking resemblance I bore to my father. I had the appearance of a studious schoolgirl, with dark brown eyes full of innocence bordering on naivety. I wore a smile that was sweet in spite of the silver of newly acquired braces. It was a picture of a child who had everything a girl her age could wish for and more. I truly was "Papa's little princess," as my father often liked to call me. Prior to the session, our photographer from Jimmy's Studio had offered retouching free of cost, to remove any blemishes or red eyes, but none had been required. The portrait was an honest depiction of what our family was: in no need of retouching and truly picture perfect.

Our maid, Sakina, cleaned the portrait every day, wiping the dust off the frame, carefully removing any cobwebs before they formed fully, and scrubbing the glass clean with her dexterous hands. Sakina's daughter, Zareen, who was only three months younger than I, would accompany her on occasion and assist her mother with the less rigorous house chores, despite my mother's opposition. She would eye the portrait with admiration and perhaps an iota of envy. When she cleaned it, I looked at her with sympathy, and the sad thought that she had to grow up without her deceased father's love.

I adored my brother, but like most siblings, we had our share of meaningless conflicts. I remember vividly when he was born and can picture the yellow Winnie-the-Pooh blanket we had bought before bringing him home from the hospital; it remained preserved in a closet of memorabilia for years. I clearly recall the first time he smiled, the first time he recognized me, and the very first time he called me *Apa*, the word for big sister. His arrival became the icing on the cake of our glorious life. His laughter echoed so loudly through the walls that I wondered sometimes if it would break them. He loved throwing and chasing after his orange ball, running after it fast as a rocket, without contemplating the perils of such an adventure, and playing with the red fire truck Papa had brought him from a trip to Europe.

My father was in the Foreign Service, and we were blessed with affluence that blinded us perhaps, to the struggles of the impoverished. My mother tastefully decorated our house, covering each wall with beautiful paintings and each floor with fancy rugs; every detail was designed to please the artistic eye. *Ammi,* as I called her, ensured that the house was meticulously clean, which was something of a challenge, considering the layers of dust that accumulated in Karachi houses. She would spend hours in the kitchen supervising the cook, making certain that the salt was just right and the flour the required consistency to be kneaded into *roti*, the perfectly circular traditional bread. She would often reassess her silverware and send Sakina periodically to have it polished.

She loved to spend time in the garden, talking to her plants, singing to them, and discussing with the gardener the bloom of the spring flowers. The pink bougainvilleas complemented the yellow in the sunflowers, so they were planted near one another. The fern appeared graceful growing up the wall and became the youngest member of the garden. The money plant had been there since my birth and had grown before my eyes, nurtured by a handful of water and few ounces of sunlight, but mostly by gallons of my mother's care. She would sometimes remove all the weeds from the garden herself, protecting her hands with thick brown gardening gloves. "Weeds spoil what's good around them," she would say, carefully and cautiously plucking out each and every one of them.

Her mothering was quite like her gardening. She would nurture us and sing to us, removing the thorns while planting roses in our paths. We were blossoming under her care, as were all the flowers in our lawn. One tight hug from her and all our petty childhood problems would evaporate, becoming absorbed into the hold of her motherly embrace. She would worry about us, like any mother, and would protect us like a bird sheltering the nest of her young. Married at the tender age of nineteen, she was very dependent on my father, which was somewhat of a cultural norm at that time in Pakistan. She did not make any decisions without his approval and seldom went out of the house unless it was to fulfill a social obligation. She was a devoted wife and mother.

She had convinced Sakina to send Zareen to school after much persuasion. Sakina was a widow who was raising her daughter alone, with some support from her deceased husband's parents. They were against sending Zareen to school, but Ammi saw what a bright girl she was and had convinced Sakina that it was sinful to deny her an education. Ammi said she would pay for it and later laid it as a condition for allowing Sakina to continue working at our home. If Zareen had any questions about her schoolwork, she came to me, and I gladly answered her queries, although she seldom needed assistance.

My father was very involved in our upbringing. He had a side that was humorous and casual and another that was mature and speculative. "These are only things, my dear," my father once said when I had accidentally broken a crystal candleholder. "Things can always be replaced. Plus, even if they are not replaced, nobody really misses them when they are gone. You must learn to love people—that's what's most important."

Papa loved to pass on his pearls of wisdom to us with every word he spoke and every action he took, setting the perfect example and yet never letting it seem like a lesson, and always sprinkling his golden words with a touch of humor. He made sure we had fun while learning.

"What does rich mean?" my brother once asked me.

"It means to have lots of money and things," had been my superficial answer.

Papa had interjected, "Let me tell you a story. There was once a scholar who had been travelling in a caravan and was looted by thieves. They said, 'Give us your money, your watch, that bag you are carrying, and your winter coat. We want everything.' The scholar proceeded to comply with their wishes and stripped himself of everything but his clothes. He did so without resistance and without becoming angry with the thieves. His friend, who was accompanying him, was surprised by his calm attitude and asked why he had agreed to give up everything so readily. 'They can take everything from me, but they cannot take from me what makes me rich, my most hard-earned and prized possession: my knowledge,' he said. What makes you rich is your soul, your knowledge; it's what's inside a person, not what's outside for everyone to see," he had said.

And the next minute we were playing Carom and card games and guessing in twenty questions. He read books to us and often took us to the library and the toy store. We would frequent the beach for mini picnics. He often became a horse for Sahir, and father and son would run and laugh uncontrollably all over the house. He checked my homework, picked me up from school, and never missed my parent-teacher meetings. If I asked for anything, I always got it, though I did not ask for much.

I once overheard my mother say to my father, "Have you ever thought that we might be spoiling Sana?" referring to me. "She always gets what she wants. She is a good girl, but what if, after she gets married, life isn't a bed of roses anymore?"

"Rubbish," my father replied. "Why do you women start thinking about marriage so soon? She is not even ten, plus I think she is already quite mature for her age. She is my little princess and she has a heart of gold. I think you and I are raising her quite well. You should stop worrying."

To stop worrying was perhaps an unreasonable expectation of a mother. I agreed with my father, though; I did not want to even think about being married. I simply wished my life to continue the same way, the problem-free life of a picture-perfect family. Who knew how my life would change a few days after this conversation took place? Who knew that the princess would fall from her throne, breaking her tiara into a million pieces and letting her heart of gold melt into a sea of sorrow?

February 11 came and it changed my life forever. I had an argument with Sahir, who had torn up the math homework that I had spent more than an hour completing. In a fit of rage, I pushed him, and he hit his mouth against the corner of the center glass table. I immediately regretted what I had done, held his hand, and took him to my mother.

"Ammi, Sahir hurt himself, he's crying." By then his upper lip was bleeding profusely, and I noticed it swelling slightly from the middle. My heart was racing, and I was saying a silent prayer: Oh, please make him better, God. Don't make him have stitches or have any broken teeth.

"Let's make it better *Beta*, she said, using the oft used endearing term for child, while disappearing into the kitchen to bring some ice. My father arrived at the scene soon after and kissed Sahir before assuming the role of investigator.

"What happened?" he inquired, looking at me.

My eyes downcast, I replied, "He hit his face on the table, Papa."

When my brother returned after having his lip treated, my father asked him if he had been jumping from the chair, which had, of late, become one of his favorite passions.

"No, Papa. Apa pushed me so hard I hit my face," he said with an angry expression, still sobbing. Papa turned to me, and guiltily I confessed to the crime.

"I am disappointed that you pushed him, but I am more disappointed that you lied to me," he said. "In this house, we only speak the truth."

Papa never raised his voice, but his words were always more powerful than the verdict of a jury. I felt ashamed. Still trying to defend myself, I argued, "I didn't lie, Papa," tears welling up in my eyes. "I just didn't tell you the whole story."

"Silence can be golden, but remember silence is as bad as a lie if it is used to hide the truth, OK, Princess?"

"I am sorry, Papa; it will not happen again. I am sorry, Sahir. You know I didn't mean to hurt you."

To cheer us up, Papa floated the idea of ice cream at Snoopy's. My mother resisted it mildly, arguing that it was cold and a school night, but her ice-cream-loving family soon outvoted her. "I want blueberry, or maybe I'll go with coconut," I said, before even reaching the destination.

"I'll have chocolate," chimed in Sahir, forgetting his injury momentarily.

I wondered what would become of my homework but pushed the thought aside. I remember vividly the taste of that ice cream (eventually I had taken both flavors), the cool wind in my face, and the old Indian song *"Bachpan kay din"* or "Days of Childhood" playing in the car on the way home, my father softly humming along with the renowned voice of Lata Mangeshkar.

The standing ritual in our home was to say goodnight and "I love you" to Ammi and Papa and thanking God for all his blessings before going to bed. The evening of February 11, I got wrapped up in redoing my homework and waited until late at night before approaching my father. He was in his study preparing for an upcoming meeting. I folded my homework neatly and put it in my bag. I was loving algebra; it all seemed to make perfect sense and was so immediately gratifying. The new version was much neater than the original one, so perhaps it was a blessing that Sahir had torn it up. Also, had he not, we might have missed out on the ice cream. Thankfully Sahir's lip did not look too bad. At least not bad enough to hurt, and hopefully not bad enough for everyone at school to notice the following morning. I was grateful that he had not torn up my English homework, which was an essay entitled "The Best Day of My Life." It would have been impossible to reproduce the same words. I had described the day when my father had returned from a long official tour. It had also been the day I had shown him my report card and he had said I made him proud and he knew that one day I would do something that would make him the proudest father of all. "You are meant to do great things," he had said.

I checked that my red-and-white uniform was pressed and my black shoes neatly polished. I checked my pencil box to make sure it had all the pencils sharpened and the pen filled with ink. We had just started using the fountain pen, and I always had marks on my hands and had to be careful not to get blue blotches on my uniform. I had already wished Ammi and Sahir good night. I still had to hug Papa, so I decided to sneak into his office and wait until after he finished his work before startling him with my hug. He was so engrossed in his papers that he did not notice me discreetly climbing under his mahogany desk.

I wondered what my father did that required him to work so many hours into the night. He often talked about his vision for our country. He once told me how many people had sacrificed their lives to build Pakistan and to finally achieve independence from the British in 1947. But this dreamland had unfortunately been plagued by lack of good leadership. Mohammad Ali Jinnah, who had been the founder of the nation, had died a year after independence was achieved and his successors had struggled to lead this new country amidst the numerous challenges that they faced. In the then-recent history, Zulfiqar Ali Bhutto's regime had been toppled by Army Chief General Zia-ul-Haq in a bloodless coup. This had occurred in July of 1977, soon after my birth. General Zia had stated that he was "totally committed to reviving democracy, and [planned to] hold fair and free elections." We do not intend to stay for long, months only, he had said, and here we were, nine years later, and he was still president. Justice must be done, he had said, and even though he denied the allegations of influencing the courts decisions, most believed that he was behind the hanging of Bhutto. My father said General Zia was taking the country in a backward direction, and he was worried about weapons and drugs coming in through the porous Afghanistan border. He had hope for Pakistan but said a lot had to change before we could make global progress.

I changed my hiding place to a more comfortable one behind the curtain, from where I could observe Papa closely. The cool night breeze was coming in through the window adjacent to the desk, which had recently been broken in by a neighbor's ball and was awaiting repair. A mug bearing the caption "All-Star Dad," which I had bought for him a year before, sat on his table, filled with tea and he was sipping from it periodically. He had removed his wallet from his pocket, and taken off his wrist -watch, and placed both of them on top of a book titled, *Immigration Laws.* He must have read three fourths of it, I thought, guessing by the placement of the bookmark that was peeking through it. I was happy to observe that the square silver ashtray, which had previously occupied a corner of the table, had moved. My mother had been working on the project of having him give up his cigars for as long as I could remember. A few days before, she had used the powerful tool of "do you want to live long and be there to see your children graduate from college? And play with your grand-children?" and it had worked like a charm. The cigars had been thrown away, and the ashtray had been reassigned a new position with other antiques on the shelf.

I would come out from behind the curtain, hug him, we would laugh together at my hiding trick, and we would all go to sleep and dream of happy things that the next sunrise would bring. Tomorrow would be marked by the usual hurried break-fast, with Sahir not finishing his milk fast enough, Ammi not get-ting the servants to do everything efficiently enough, and Papa not getting to read the newspaper quick enough. Then would come school, which meant seeing Amna, my other friends, and my teachers, all of whom I adored. I was hoping I would get a star for my redone homework. I had studied the spellings for the test the next morning because I had to get them all right, including "receive" and "relieve," which always confused me, in order to make my parents proud. The many imperfections would define the perfect day ahead.

My thoughts were interrupted by a loud bang, which ripped through my ears like a volcano. I was paralyzed with fear and tried to scream, but my voice was strangled in my throat before it could reach my lips. My heart was racing, and my head was pounding fast, as if it were about to explode. At first I could not comprehend what was happening. Perhaps it was a loud storm? No, it was too loud and too near, just like the television show the week before, in which the police and the criminals had been shooting each other. This had to be the sound of a gun. Someone had given Sahir a toy gun for his third birthday, and Papa had thrown it away. He had refused to have an armed security guard deployed at our gate; that was how much he despised guns. It was dark behind the curtain, and it suddenly seemed like there was no air.

Finding all the courage I could muster, I came out from behind the curtain and witnessed the worst horror of my life. My father was sprawled on the floor like a helpless child, a bullet in his chest, his starched white shirt covered in a sea of blood. He moaned slightly and then closed his eyes. It was as if he had fallen into a restful sleep. I will never know if he saw me there, whether he felt pain, whether he knew that that was the end. I looked at him in disbelief. This must be a dream, a really bad dream that needed to end. Why wouldn't someone wake me up? Where was everyone? Ammi, Sakina, Zareen—someone please wake me up. I need to wake up and get ready for school. Papa will drop me on his way to work. I have a spelling test in the first period.

But it was not a dream. It was a harsh reality, rather, and one that would redefine my existence. I did not know whether to cry or scream or run or hug my father's lifeless body. Who could do this? My father was a loving, giving soul, always doing good in this world—helping the poor, fighting for human rights, preaching the mantra of peace, setting the example of virtue. Who could possibly want him dead? He had refused to have an armed guard, despite my mother's insistence. He said, "Does that mean the person protecting me should take a bullet for me? Wouldn't that mean that my life is more precious than his? Every life is equally important, isn't it?"

I could not breathe. And then I caught a glimpse of a face in the window, the window broken by the cricket ball. The memory of this face would haunt me for a long time. The details of his features would be engraved in my mind forever, much like an ineradicable imprint on a fossil: the square face, the diagonal scar covering a broad forehead, the brown, unkempt hair, the stubble, and the cold, green, merciless eyes. They were the eyes of a killer, my father's killer, the eyes of my worst enemy, and I would never forget them. This was my unbreakable promise to my father and to myself. He was pure evil, this man who had taken my father away from me before he had even had the last sip of his tea, before I had had the chance to hug him good night, and before he had been able to call me his princess once again.

Chapter 2

I was still in shock when I saw my mother running into the room. I was sweating profusely. I tried to speak but was unable to articulate any words. Sakina and the other servants had been awoken by the noise and had come running in as well. What followed was a series of shouts and screams, with one person calling for a doctor and another saying the word "dead" and then "he is no more." Much of that moment is blurred in my memory even though the emotions it evoked are still vivid. I remember Papa's face, white as a ghost, and his white shirt covered in the deepest hue of crimson. My father's blood was everywhere: on the beige carpet, on the wall, on the family portrait across the desk. Another bullet must have hit the portrait too, for the glass that covered it was shattered into several pieces that lay strewn across the study. No one realized that I had been there all that time or that I had seen my father take his last breath and heard his last moan. They did not know that I had seen the person who had committed this heinous crime. Ammi saw me there and assumed that I had just arrived after being woken up by the commotion. She attempted to cover my eyes and held me in a tight hug. That embrace was the balm I needed, but within minutes I felt my mother's arms loosen from around me. At that precise moment, I felt her hug vanish, as if her protection had suddenly left me. I looked up and realized that she had fainted. In another room, Sahir was in a deep sleep, surrounded by teddy bears beneath a ceiling covered with glowing stars, peacefully dreaming of a beautiful tomorrow.

My father was "no more," pronounced the physician who was called in. How could that be? We had just had ice cream. Minutes ago he had been there, seated at his desk, trying to make the world a better place. His mug was still warm from his last sip of unconsumed tea, and the bookmark remained trapped on page 142 of his unfinished book.

How could my papa be gone already? I was not even ten. How could I bear to live my life without him? And what about Sahir, robbed of his father before his fifth birthday, before he could truly understand what a special person his dad was? What would become of my mother, my thirty-year-old beautiful mother, not wise in the ways of the world? She was now a widow. As disbelief transitioned into grief, the tears came and fell like a torrential rainfall.

When Ammi was composed enough to speak again, a few hours after having regained consciousness, she said, "We don't need Sahir to know how it happened, dear. He is too young to understand. We just need to tell him your father is in *jannat*," referring to the Urdu word for Heaven. "God loved him so much that he chose him to be with him in a better place."

Yes, Sahir was too young for all this. But what about me? How was I expected to comprehend that my father had been killed in cold blood? How was I to bear all this pain and not even be able to share it with my only sibling? I almost told Ammi that I had seen the killer but did not want to upset her more, so I let it be. I buried it inside me along with all the other sad realities that were signing up to become my lifelong companions.

Ammi suddenly looked like she had aged. She was sad and unsure, like a child who had forgotten the way home. She had lost her husband, and with him, she had lost the only life she had ever known. She tried her best to comfort me, but I soon realized that I had to grow up quickly so I could take care of her and protect her.

I cannot remember when I went to sleep, but that marked the beginning of my nightmares. Sometimes I dreamt of my father lying before me in a pool of blood and I would wake up screaming. On other occasions I only saw his killer, with his green, evil eyes staring at me and threatening to kill me as well. Frequently I was also covered in blood, unable to wipe it off me. I would try to scream, but my voice could not be heard. Then I would wake up, my hands clammy with cold sweat, my heart pounding with fear. The dreams were always gruesome and vivid, and they were so disturbing that I was afraid to fall asleep. I had heard of people sleeping for days after tragedies like this one so they could dull the pain and pretend temporarily that none of it was real, but I had no way to escape it. I slept next to my mother for several days, and she would wake up, gently put her hand on my forehead, and give me a glass of water to drink. But she herself was so distraught that she could not find words effective enough to comfort me. In the mornings, I would find her pillow wet from all the tears that had trickled down her cheeks the night before. After a few weeks, the dreams became less frequent, but whenever they came, they came with a vengeance.

Zareen helped for several days while Sakina tended to all the other housekeeping responsibilities. One day, she saw me crying in my room, and brought me a glass of lemon juice. Referring to her own father, she said, "Abba died when I was four. I was as old as Sahir is now. I remember him a little bit, but not a lot. I am very sad about your papa. He was a very kind man."

She had said what others had shied away from. Her words gave me comfort and let me know that someone shared my pain and cared enough to express it.

One morning when the house was eerily quiet and many of the relatives who had travelled long distances to offer condolences were gone, I was lying with my head in my mother's lap when she said, "I want you and Sahir to go with Phuppo to California for a few months to get away from all this. It's been so tough for you; you need a change." Phuppo was what we called our Aunt Asma, my father's only sister.

"What about you, Ammi?" I asked. "I don't want to leave you alone."

"I cannot go because I have to remain in the house for another three and a half months, as our religion and culture dictate," she replied, "but you and Sahir must go."

Sensing my worry and hesitation, she held my hand and said, "Besides, I won't be alone, your Nana will stay here."

I was comforted by the thought that my grandfather would be there with my mother. Before we knew it, our bags were packed and we were on the twenty-two-hour flight to California with my aunt. Initially I had not welcomed this idea. I believed that after suffering such an unthinkable loss, the family should stay together. I needed my mother, and she needed me. She had been right, however, in saying that she could not leave for the period of *'Iddat'* of four months and ten days, and she did not want us to become homebound because of her, especially in a house full of Papa. Everywhere, there were memories of him: his voice, his humming of old Lata songs, his casual flipping of the pages of the morning newspaper. I looked at the new metallic glasses that had arrived in the mail after his death, the ones he had ordered at my insistence. I could not bear it. The carpet stain remained, a brutal reminder of what had taken place, despite countless attempts to remove it. The portrait frame had been rubbed clean by Sakina. What about the blood oozing from my heart? When would that stop? The glass on the picture could be replaced, but what about all the cracks inside my being? The laceration in my heart was deep and wide, and it was bleeding. Healing this wound would take a long time and would be sure to leave a permanent scar—a scar that would always hurt and would be there for all to see. I soon welcomed the idea of escaping, of going to a place where I did not see pity in people's eyes, pity for a little princess who had lost her king.

Within a week of our departure, Ammi called me to inform me that the murderer had been arrested. I thought to myself that the killer being caught would not bring back my father, but despite that, this knowledge gave me some sense of justice, a hint of peace amid all the restlessness inside me. Whatever punishment was granted to him would never be equivalent to the unthinkable crime he had committed. Even if he were shot in the chest a hundred times, it would not take my pain away.

"Why did he do it?" I asked matter-of-factly.

"For money," she replied. "He took your father's money and his watch. He had to run away quickly because everyone heard the gunshot."

I could not help but think of what my father used to say: "These are things. Never cry over them, never fight with others for them. The happiness things bring does not last, and people think that when the happiness fades, they need more things, not realizing that it's not going to last either, because this kind of happiness doesn't touch the soul."

Papa had lost his life to someone's greed, someone's love for these material things. Did this killer have no one to tell him that things can be bought, that they can be replaced, but that no price could be put on human life?

In California, I felt somewhat alone in my pain and suffering because I was separated by oceans from my mother and my brother was too young for any discussions about what had transpired that winter. I was envious of him because he had not witnessed what I had, and he was unaware of the horrendous way in which Papa had died. He missed him but simply believed that he had gone to a faraway land called *jannat*. He could not, at that age, comprehend the permanence of this separation, the finality of death.

My aunt was a maternal figure who had my father's generosity and integrity. She also bore a striking resemblance to him, the identical chiseled nose and the same wide, generous smile.

She had lived in the States ever since her marriage to my uncle, whom we called Phuppa. He was an accountant by profession, and had a quiet and polite demeanor. As my father had said, "There are two kinds of people in this world, those who give and those who take. Always be a giver, my dear." I believed I could clearly classify my uncle as a giver. Time taught me that my father's black and white description was an oversimplification for the purposes of my understanding, of the many shades of gray that people really were. Time also taught me that my early impression of Phuppa was an accurate one.

Phuppo was an enormous support during those dark days when I first arrived. She would hold me, imparting all the love she had perhaps saved up for years for children of her own, which sadly she had not been able to have. She once advised me to talk about my father, rather than pretending that everything was normal and that there had been no loss. It would help the healing process, she explained. It was good advice, and I took it; I started asking her about my father's childhood, as I had always loved to hear him narrate those tales himself. She told me about my paternal grandparents who had died many years ago. She described how my grandmother loved to sew and how she also loved to sing when no one was listening. She told me how my grandfather had been involved in the freedom movement in his early days. She talked about the home of their childhood, the garden filled with mango trees, and how she and Papa would climb up the branches and try to get as many mangoes as they could. Soon my aunt and I became very close.

One night she heard me screaming in my sleep and came running to my bedroom. She held me tight and asked me if I had had a bad dream. I told her about it and how it had become a recurrent nightmare, censoring the part about the killer. She hugged me, and it felt reassuring to be hugged again.

On Memorial Day weekend, my uncle announced that we were going to San Francisco. April had been a crazy time owing to tax return season, and until then none of us had felt emotionally ready for sightseeing. Before we knew it, we were at the Golden Gate Bridge, walking alongside the youngsters on their bicycles, the cool wind blowing our hair away, the soft drizzle wetting our faces. We took pictures from every angle, trying to capture the intricate details. It looked stunningly beautiful, bursting with life. I was later shocked to learn that many had committed suicide by jumping off this breathtaking bridge.

We visited Crooked Street, where I had to hold Sahir's hand tight so he would not go down the innumerable stairs too fast. We spent some time at Pier 39, and Sahir was delighted by the way he could mimic the sounds of the sea lions who lay motionless on the boards that floated above the water. We sat on the Merry-go-round, and it was difficult to convince Sahir to dismount the carousel, with its dragons, dolphins, and countless horses. The evening concluded with a sumptuous clam chowder soup served in a sourdough bread bowl. I had heard of all these places from my father, who had travelled the world. Everywhere I went, I thought of him and how his feet had touched the same ground. I would start to smile, but every time I let joy near, I felt guilty, as if happiness was disrespectful to my father's memory. I was unable to get two images out of my mind: one of my father and the other of his ruthless killer. My hatred for the killer was so intense, that it almost seemed to overpower my love for my father. The image of Papa lying there like a helpless child had cast a shadow on all the good memories of our happy past. The horrific moment that played in my mind like a video set on replay. One moment had become more powerful than nine and a half years.

Our spring visit was extended to the summer. I was missing a lot of school, but Phuppo assured me that I would catch up. But before the school year began, I returned to my parents' home, where my widowed mother needed me. Sahir asked me on the long flight if Papa was back from his trip to *Jannat*. I had to swallow tears as I told him that it was a really long trip and it was the best place to be in. He asked me if we could go there to visit him, and I said I did not think so. I always wondered when it was that Sahir understood that Papa was never coming back. It was a question that he never asked, and one I never answered.

My brother and I came back to a home that bore little resemblance to the one we had left behind. The lights that had illuminated the exterior of the house had all been turned off. The decorations, pictures, and even our family portrait in the office were gone. The furniture was sparse, the plants and flowers were mostly dead, and those that were still alive had lost their freshness. There were countless brown cardboard boxes of various sizes stacked on top of one another in a disorganized fashion, some sealed with tape and all labeled in thick, black permanent ink. The stifling smell of emptiness permeated the air. Sahir was excited to see all the cartons, and immediately started jumping from one to another like an acrobat who had found props, while I felt dizzy and struggled to overcome the nausea I was starting to feel.

The gardener and the cook were gone. Sakina was still there and greeted me warmly, but her expression was peculiar. She started talking fast about the heavy rains, our long flight, the worsening power outages, and Zareen's recent encounter with malaria. It seemed as though she were trying to establish a false sense of normalcy.

Amid the piles of cardboard boxes stood my mother, who appeared to be a different woman. She looked nothing like herself, instead resembled the wilted flowers in her garden. The color from her face had vanished, and dark circles underlined her morose eyes. Her hair was tied into a braid, and a premature hint of gray was visible on her scalp. She wore no makeup or jewelry. The woman who had been so conscious of the cut of her dress and the style of her shoes stood before me in a plain brown cotton suit with slippers on her feet, which I had never before seen without nail polish. She had always had her wrist decorated with a bracelet and each finger bejeweled with a ring, but her hands were now bare. She appeared thin, and her clothes hung loose on her shoulders. Her face was gaunt, robbed of the rosy cheeks that once were and devoid of the smile that had been capable of taking all my sorrow away. Was this really my mother? It seemed like my father had taken her with him. She was a body without a person inside. That was the powerful instant when I realized that my father was not the only one I had lost on that dreaded night.

The morning after we returned, Ammi said we had to go for a walk in the garden. The last time we had gone for a walk in the garden was when my mother had informed me of my grandmother's death. Suddenly I felt fearful; she could not possibly have any more bad news to give me. She had lost so much weight. Was she ill? Could she be dying too?

"We have to discuss something important," she said, grown-up stuff that I, the now ten-year-old big girl, would understand.

"Are you all right? You aren't ill, are you? Do you have cancer or something?" I asked, my whole body trembling.

"No, Sana. I am fine."

I was so relieved that I took a deep breath and felt grateful that there was nothing she could say that could possibly upset me.

Her voice was shaking slightly when she started. "*Beta,*" she said, "this has all been very difficult for all of us, especially you and me: being without your dad, the way it happened, being alone. Being alone is very hard, and in our society it is very tough for a woman without a husband. Nana has decided what's best for all of us."

She paused, all the while nervously biting her nails and avoiding looking at me directly. So what had my grandfather decided? Papa had made the decisions, and now Nana was making the decisions.

"He thinks I should remarry."

And there it was, plain and simple. This was the grown-up stuff I was supposed to understand, gulp it down like a sip of bitter medicine. My life was turning in many unexpected directions, full of uneven gravel and a multitude of speed bumps; but now it seemed to have reached a dead end.

"He is a nice man, educated and kind, and he has agreed to marry me and to adopt both of you and raise you as his children. He was previously married, but things didn't work out. There are not many men in our culture who would agree to take on such a big responsibility."

I looked at her with disbelief, trying to find the right words. "But why, Ammi? You won't be alone if I am with you and Sahir is with you. And Nana can live with us. Why do you need to get married? Papa has barely been in his grave; it hasn't even been six months. How can you do this? Sakina's husband died five years ago and she has not remarried. Why do you have to..." my voice trailed off as I realized how pointless my questions were. I was not being asked, I was being told. The decision had been made, and the date of the wedding had been agreed upon and printed on an invitation card. It was the date that Papa would be replaced by a stranger and the date that I would lose the only thing I had left of my father: his name.

"Anyway we had to leave the house. It was a government-allotted house through your father's job. They will take it away, along with the car and the domestic staff."

I glanced over at the two sunflowers that seemed to have survived the storm in our lives and envied the bird that still sung her song. So my mother had brought me here to gently tell me that my life was over. "Where will we go?" I asked in a tone of resignation.

"To your new papa's home," she replied matter-of-factly. "It's not as big or as luxurious, but it is a decent-sized new home not far from here."

Now I understood the boxes and my prolonged visit to my aunt's. I couldn't believe my mother was talking to me about the size of our new house as if it mattered to me. Had the new residence been Buckingham Palace, I would not have wanted to leave my home; it was all I had left of my father's memories. This was where my childhood was, where Sahir had been born, where laughter had once echoed through the walls, where Papa had taken his last breath. Where Zareen had been given the gift of education. Where happiness had prevailed. And the car was going too. It was the car in which I had gone places with my father, where we had listened to our favorite songs and eaten delicious ice cream. The front seat still had the scent of his cologne.

So Ammi was going to marry someone else. How could she? How could she forget Papa so soon? How could she replace him with someone else? "Your new papa," she had said with such ease. I could not bear it. I went to my room, buried my face in the pillow, and wept until the early hours of dawn.

Chapter 3

I did not wish to speak to my mother or my grandfather, who I held partly responsible for planning the wedding behind my back. I had been close to Nana and I failed to comprehend how he could have made a decision that was so deeply hurtful to me in every possible way. He had taught me so much about life, reading stories to me and explaining the morals behind each of them, that his actions seemed hypocritical and unfair.

"It's all for the better," Nana said, putting his arm around me. He placed his teacup with its saucer back on the glass table, and insisted I take some cookies he had kept aside for me. I refused the sugar-sprinkled Nice Biscuits with a wave of my hand. He was going home for a few days to take care of household matters after having stayed with my mother for all these months. "I know you are upset now, but you will see many years later, when you are old enough to understand things, that this really is the best thing for everyone involved. You need to have a father figure, a man of the house. And he is a nice person; he will treat you all well. If you are nice to him, he will be good to you too. He will be just like your real father."

"No one can be like my real father," I replied, my voice raised and my tone harsh.

"My father is in heaven. You just said that this man would be nice to us if we were nice to him. Papa was nice to us even if we were disobedient. He loved us on all the days, even when we were rascals. That's why a stepfather is a stepfather. And many years later, *you* will see that." I could not believe I had been so defiant in my tone to my grandfather, and deep inside I started to develop a dislike for my new self. This was not me, the well-mannered girl my parents had been raising me to be. But it was as if he did not have any idea of the emotional turmoil he was causing. I left him standing alone at the door with his cane, without assisting him down the three stairs that led to the outside. I could not help noticing how frail he had become, how he had to pause between words to catch his breath, and how the wrinkles on his face seemed to have become suddenly darker and deeper, and how there seemed to be so much effort hiding behind his smile. His daughter's widowhood had been an unthinkable tragedy that had befallen him at this difficult age when arthritis had settled in his knees and impaired his walking somewhat, when vision was not as clear, and hearing not as sharp as his younger days. I felt a pang of sympathy for him, realizing that he too was a victim of this misfortune that had come into our lives. That emotion was strong enough to overcome the anger I felt for the devastating decision he had taken for me.

My mother had not talked much to me since the day she had broken this news to me. I was angry with her but had not had a chance to express it to her. She had purposely been hiding behind the shield of wedding preparations to avoid an unpleasant confrontation with me. Sure, my grandfather had a major part in this, but as my father had always said, everyone is responsible for his or her own actions. He was not forcing my mother to remarry; ultimately it was her saying the three-letter affirmative that was about to change all our lives.

The wedding was a simple affair. My mother wore a solemn expression yet somehow looked beautiful again. My stepfather was in real estate, and everyone called him Mr. Rehman. He was tall and somewhat stocky with a carefully trimmed black moustache; he had the appearance of a rather proper gentleman. However, even if he had he been the greatest humanitarian with the most generous heart, I could not have done anything except despise him. My hatred for my stepfather was nearly as intense as that for Papa's killer with the cold green eyes. No one in this world could replace my father—not in the family portrait, not in my home, and certainly not in my heart.

"For the official adoption, your names will now be Sana and Sahir Rehman," my mother had informed me as if it were part of a newscast. Not Sana Asad Shah, but Sana Rehman: the new me. I felt like my identity was slowly disintegrating, and there was nothing I could do to prevent it. Sahir, on the other hand, seemed to be adjusting quite well to the new situation. He was bonding with our new papa and they seemed to easily form a father-son relationship. He even managed to bring a smile to the very serious Mr. Rehman's face on occasion. I saw Sahir playing cricket with him, laughing and chatting, not noticing me at all, not seeming to feel Papa's absence at all, and I realized an important reality: I was alone.

Whenever my mother was with my stepfather, I would turn away; I could not bear to see Ammi with anyone other than Papa. I had not yet come to terms with my father having passed away and already had to deal with a new man in her life. She had always been a people pleaser, but I had never thought this trait would become a drawback and take her further away from me. She was forever trying to please her new husband, making us do everything in accordance with his house rules. It seemed as though he had done us all a favor by marrying my widowed mother and assuming responsibility of her two children.

I struggled to adjust. Every few days I would think of my father's killer and how he had ruined my entire life. I imagined visiting him in prison and telling him what he had done. I tried to get a hold of the newspaper, but somehow everyone managed to hide it from me. I had read the obituary announcing my father's death, but I was sheltered from all subsequent news updates. I overheard my grandfather say "life imprisonment" and wondered why they would not execute a person who had committed such an unforgivable crime. Perhaps it was better this way; if he died now, he would not suffer. I wanted him to suffer, to never see the breaking of dawn or the fall of dusk. I wanted him to never taste the freshness of a home-cooked meal, never enjoy the smell of grass, and never feel the miraculous touch of a raindrop. I wanted him to pine for the sound of music, and be deafened by the sound of silence. I wished for him to feel nothing but the nagging pain of loneliness. I wanted him to forever remain behind those metal bars, separated permanently from those he loved, to only dream of a freedom that would never be attainable, and to live every moment of a long life in repentance.

I was not allowed to talk about my father or even put a picture of him in my room, as it might upset my new papa. My father was gone, but I would not let his memories be buried with him. I thought of running away but realized that was irrational. I was a child; where would I go? Nana would not be able to take care of me, plus he had been behind all of this to begin with. Maybe I could go live with Amna. After all, she seemed like my only ally and she was my best friend. We were in the same class, so we could come and go to school together without too much inconvenience to anybody. I floated the idea in school, and she was overwhelmed with excitement; she said of course I could live with her, why not? But her parents were my mother's friends and would never agree to anything that would upset her. Plus going off and living at a friend's house while your own home was two streets down would be crossing social boundaries. Even as a child, cultural norms and expectations had seeped into my psyche.

Still, I knew I simply had to leave, to go to a place where I did not have to see my stepfather next to my mother, where I did not have to put up with his presence every morning of every day. A thought came to mind, and I decided to write a letter to Phuppo.

"Dear Phuppo,

Salam. Hope you are well. Ever since we returned from California, things have been horrible. You know how much I loved Papa, I can't bear to see my mother married again. I tried, I really tried, because Nana asked me to, and Ammi begged me to, but my stepfather is mean and I am pretty sure he hates me. I told him that I wouldn't call him Papa or Abbu, and he got so angry, he started yelling at me and Ammi. I can't even talk about Papa. The pictures I have of him are in my drawer. I don't even know where our family picture is hidden. No one mentions Papa, it's as if he never existed. I cannot live like this. I loved Papa and I love you, you are just like him. I think you are the only one who is still on my side. Can I please move to California? Can I please live with you? Ammi doesn't know that I am writing you this letter. Please write soon.

Love,
Your niece, Sana."

I asked Sakina to have it mailed so no one would become suspicious; it was the most conniving thing I had ever done. Mail in those days was slow and unreliable, so I waited for a few weeks patiently hoping and praying. I was sure she would want me to live with her, but I was not sure about Phuppa. The letter came in a big white envelope and I rushed to tear it open. She wrote that she would be more than happy to take me in, that she had discussed it with Phuppa, and that I would be like the daughter they had never had. I had US citizenship, so I did not require a visa. She wrote that it would significantly help her deal with her loss, as she would feel like a part of her brother was with her. That was what I wanted—to be in a place where my father was remembered, where his praises were sung, where his pictures graced the walls, where missing him did not require an apology, and where his name did not top the unspoken list of prohibited words.

My mother was upset at me for my audacity and at my aunt for supporting my unreasonable demands. They had been close previously, but my mother's new marriage so soon after my father's passing had created some understandable resentment between them. My mother was weak, however, and soon gave in to the idea. It seemed that part of her was relieved; she and her new husband had by then started quarrelling rather frequently, and I was the central theme of all their arguments. I often overheard my mother asking him to give me some more time.

"She will adjust; please give her one more chance. She's really not usually rude like that, she just..." Her tone was that of someone begging for mercy, knowing that it was unlikely to be granted. Mr. Rehman was a decent man but had a sizable ego, and he could not tolerate my impertinent behavior or my refusal to call him papa or abbu. My mother was struggling to make her marriage work. If things fell apart, she would have nowhere to go. I wished I could take my baby brother with me. After all I was not angry with him—envious maybe, but not angry. He was a child and he did what he was told. If he got along well with my stepfather, then that was probably good for him. I knew deep inside that he could not go with me. I was the one having trouble with everything, not him. Being separated from him was the price I would have to pay for my freedom.

I asked to go to the beach, where Papa used to take us every weekend. I loved to collect seashells and had collected several of them, which I kept in a jar at home. Papa would often put a large shell to his ear and show us how to hear the sound of the ocean through it. I took a small container with me and filled it with some sand. Papa always used to tell me how people would take the sand of their homeland with them whenever they left so they did not lose the connection with their country. I visited my school, where I had been since kindergarten; it was where I had spent memorable times and made the best of friends, where I had helped paint a wall with a rainbow and plant a tree that was now several feet tall, where my biggest worry had been being three minutes late for school and missing the morning assembly, where I had cut my forehead after falling from the swing and had learned to recite the national anthem with fervor. It was where I had spent one rupee each day on a tiny packet of mouthwatering chili chips that burnt the tongue yet had the power of addicting us all. It was where Amna and I had discovered a secret hiding place near a staircase that no one else knew about, and where the red-bearded man we called "Lala" had conscientiously banged the metal drum to signal the ending of every half-hour period.

I asked to see my old house before leaving, as it was the only home I had ever known, each wall housing a remembrance, every corner telling a story. It was vacant now, filled with hard-working men redoing the paint on the walls. It had a strong smell of fresh paint, but strongest of all was the scent of unfamiliarity. I spent a few moments in my room, reflecting on the last time I had had a restful sleep in my bed. Then I proceeded to the study, where, despite the newspapers lining the floors and the spatter of ivory paint all over, I could still feel my father's presence. I gazed up at the newly installed window, while saying a silent prayer. I promised Papa that I would always keep his memory alive. I vowed never to forget him or all that he had taught me in the small serving of time he had been given to share with me.

On the way back, we passed the bookstore where I had spent time with my father and had sought his advice about which book to read next. We also went by the bakery where Sahir and I had munched on countless lemon pastries and hundreds of cookies made of toasted coconut. I did not realize then that I would miss it all: the speed breakers that punctuated the road, the vendors selling fresh guavas accompanied by the traditional *masala,* the heavily decorated buses weaving through the chaotic traffic.

After returning to my mother's new house, I glanced at the painting that we had moved from our old house and remembered with fondness the comparison Papa had drawn to it with our family. My father was the mountain that stood tall and protected us from the harshness of the world beyond, while cementing us together. My mother was the tree providing us with cool shade, shielding us from the scorching sun. My brother was the many flowers, bright and colorful, bringing life and spreading joy. I was the lake beneath, tranquil and content. Little had he known that I would become the lone bird flying away far into the distance.

Ammi helped me pack my things with tears in her eyes; it seemed she did not quite know what to say. She insisted I take several sets of the traditional *shalwar kameez*, many of which she had asked the tailor to stitch for me in a hurry immediately after my plans had been finalized. She wanted to make sure I did not forget my roots. She also slipped in a *janamaz,* or prayer rug, and a book with some verses from the Quran and quotations of Prophet Muhammad.

"Don't forget how to speak Urdu," she said. I was surprised she could even contemplate the thought of me forgetting my mother tongue. She had forgotten her loving husband so quickly and had made all traces of him disappear with such ease, yet she was worried about my severed ties with my country and my language. The way she was bidding me farewell made it seem as though I was going for good. That is what I had asked for, so why did her farewell advice make me so despondent? I realized now that a part of me had wanted her to stop me. I probably would have declined, but the heaviness in my heart may have been lightened a bit. I had had a dream a few nights before my flight that I was leaving and my mother stood at the door, begging me not to go. But it was just a dream, and this time it was a dream I did not ask to wake up from. After all, I was the weed that had to be plucked out, carefully and cautiously, or I would ruin the good around me in my mother's new garden.

I did not care about which clothes or shoes I would leave behind; I just asked for the "All-Star Dad" mug and the family portrait, which was now devoid of the protective glass that had covered it but retained the bronze frame bordering it. It was a depiction of what my family had been, the embodiment of happiness and unsurpassable harmony, all of us fitting together like pieces of a jigsaw puzzle. All of us posing for a picture, under direction of a professional photographer, the smiles on celluloid a precise translation of the joy within.

The portrait was now merely a glimpse of what my life had been, simply a memory I was packing in my suitcase next to all my other tangible belongings: my hairbrush, my books and my pair of faded blue jeans.

Chapter 4

I arrived in Freemont after what seemed like an endless flight. I had tried not to think about the horror of my recent past, the unpredictability of my future, or whether or not I was making wise choices for myself. I drowned myself in *Jane Eyre*, which I had shoved at the last minute into my carry-on luggage. Within minutes of landing, I immediately sensed a warm welcome and felt reassured that I had made the right decision. Asma Phuppo and Phuppa beamed with delight as they saw me emerge from the crowd at San Francisco Airport.

In their house, my room had been arranged with considerable care. One wall was lined with a wooden shelf filled with books for me to read, while another had a stereo set up for me to enjoy songs of my choice. The room was painted an apple green, my favorite color, and a light but cozy comforter with green and purple flowers covered the bed. Everything was new and fresh, and more importantly, it had all been prepared especially for me. This was my new abode, my escape from my past life. I loved my aunt and uncle, and they did the best they could to fill the void within me. I had had a terrible thing happen to me, but it seemed that my childhood would bear no resemblance to that of Jane Eyre's.

I embraced my new home, as I did my new family. I resembled my aunt more than I did my mother, and that helped make the transition smoother. Phuppo worked part time and had rearranged her schedule to fit in with my school hours. She was motherly and affectionate, showering all the love that she had saved up inside her. The only thing she needed to work on was ensuring that my braids were even and symmetric, and that my parting was straight enough to match my mother's skilful hand. My uncle seemed pleased with my presence, regularly bringing home my favorite chocolates and borrowing books from the library after thoroughly researching what I liked, but it took him several months to assume the parental role. It gave me enough time to ease into my new surroundings, to gain the confidence of opening the refrigerator as I pleased, and use the telephone for long distance calls as I wished. Everything seemed very quiet at first. My aunt and uncle were accustomed to the silence, having suffered through the pain of childlessness for a decade. They had accepted this life for themselves and had welcomed me as the bloom of an unseen spring in their empty garden.

There were hardly ever any guests, especially not uninvited ones. Neighbors did not randomly knock on one another's doors, although everyone was very cordial and rather meticulous about waving hello. One did not wake up to the sacred sound of the *Fajr Azaan*, the call for prayer signaling the break of dawn. One could not hear the loud water tankers barging in through the gates at early hours of the morning, as I had been used to, or the doorbell ringing for the newspaper man, followed shortly by the milkman, who was regularly admonished for the declining quality of the milk he delivered. One could not hear the sound of crows that invariably found their way onto the grill-covered windowpanes or the soft singing of the *koyal*, which dominated the skies in the mango season, arriving promptly in the middle of every May. The night did not end with the shrill whistle of the street watchman reassuring all of his presence and wakefulness. Most of all, there was no Sahir to chase after, argue with, or laugh uncontrollably with. I regretted all the times I had yelled at him for being too loud and not letting me complete my homework, watch my favorite television show, or simply have some peace and quiet.

The weather was not too different from that in Karachi; it was mostly hot and sunny, except for the evenings, which were several degrees cooler. Also, indoors one seldom felt the wrath of the heat, owing to air-conditioning that was both effective and ubiquitous. My aunt would always ensure that I took my jacket along or an extra layer of clothing, as well as an umbrella, to protect myself from the unpredictable cold and rainfall. We were often invited to dinners on weekends, mostly at the houses of Pakistani families, where the socializing was pleasant but more extensive and formal than what I was accustomed to.

On weekdays, everything was dead quiet. I was hesitant to walk to and from the restroom at night, afraid that the creaking of the wooden floors would wake my uncle from his restful sleep. In the mornings, I welcomed the rhythmic rumble of the dishwasher and the sound of Michael mowing his lawn next door. They were both effective at overpowering the incessant ticking of the wall clocks that served as reminders of the overly scheduled life I was living. The aroma of freshly cooked *roti* off the *tawa* had been replaced by the scent of lemony cleaners and lavender fabric softeners. I liked America, I enjoyed school, and I spent a great amount of time reading and trying to put the past behind me. But it seemed that no matter how fast I tried to run from it, it always caught up with me.

The thought of the lethal bullet that took my father's life followed me like a tall, dark shadow. Once, on my way back from school in the bus, I was immersed in my usual deep thoughts of that haunting night and missed my stop. I was sitting in a corner at the back, and no one realized that I had forgotten to get off. Phuppo was frantic with worry, crying inconsolably when my school principal informed her that I was all right and that I had gone back to school. When she came to pick me up, she gave me a tight hug and held on to me for several minutes, as though she had found a lost treasure. I felt guilty for putting her through such unnecessary agony, but she responded with something she often said: "All's well that ends well." From that day, I made a conscious effort to free myself from being consumed by the demon of my terrifying memories.

I acutely felt some of the cultural differences, which required some adjustment but made me understand that there were many kinds of individuals in this world. Meeting people from various countries and religious backgrounds made me realize that despite the differences, fundamentally everyone was the same: at the end of the day, we were all human beings who needed love and craved peace.

I tried to hold on to my roots while allowing my branches to spread far and high into the sky. I met many people who were foreign to this land, like myself, and had faced the greater challenge of having to learn English, which fortunately for us had been the medium of teaching in many schools. This had been the minuscule compensation for having endured the British regime for decades prior to achieving independence in August of 1947. Our ancestors had made sacrifices to earn their rights, and thanks to their efforts, we had been born free in a nation where learning English was encouraged. Like all foreigners, I struggled to blend in while preserving my core ingredients, hoping to create an amalgam that was both flavorful and genuine. I struggled to protect my conservative values from undergoing an unconscious fermentation while trying to adapt all the virtues of the modernized, western world. I quickly became familiar with the term "ABCD," an abbreviation for American-Born Confused Desi, which referred to Indian and Pakistani children who were being raised in America. I met a myriad of people in school who had stepparents and broken homes. I empathized with them, and they with me. In Pakistan I had felt like no one could understand what I had gone through, as second marriages there were rare even after untimely deaths and divorces were almost nonexistent. It was a time when mothers told their daughters that they had to "burn their boats" so there was no possibility of returning back to their parents once they were married. Things were changing there too, gradually, of course.

Nevertheless, I had somehow not known of any child my age having to endure what I had. In America I had met girls and boys in worse situations, children with parents who divorced because after a few years they had simply started hating each other or they had decided they loved another person or that they had married the wrong person. They were shuffled from mother to father and stepmother to stepfather, becoming characters in courtroom dramas and pawns in ugly custody battles. They had their lives put on schedules for every weekend and every holiday. I heard their stories, shared their pain, and lent them my shoulder to cry on. I told them my story, carefully editing the circumstances surrounding my father's death. None of the accounts were the same—they each had a different beginning and a unique conclusion—but they all had the common theme of the abandoned child who was being punished for the decisions of his or her parents.

I tried to block out the dreaded night from my mind. The dreams continued, however, and each time waking me with a jolt, a cruel reminder of the past that often crept into the present. My aunt insisted that I seek counseling to help the night terrors dissipate, but I adamantly refused, not wanting to discuss what I had seen. Phuppo never pushed too hard for anything, resigning often to my defiance but reassuring me that she was always there to help me.

I avoided thinking about my mother or her new union. Part of me loved her for being the wonderful mother she had been, and part of me hated her for callously stepping off that pedestal. I could not forgive her for tearing my family apart or for asking me to call a stranger my father. I could not forget that she had forced me to change my name and lose my identity.

I missed Sahir terribly and often thought of him and the sound of his giggles, the fuss he made over finishing his glass of milk, and our petty arguments. I remembered how angry I became when anyone else bothered him, how I always took on the big sister role and fought for him. And now I had come to the other side of the world, leaving him to fight for himself. I shared my feelings with Phuppo, and she and I agreed that we would have Sahir come visit every winter. I could go in the summers, and he could come in the winters; this way, we could spend our holidays together. Tickets were expensive, and travelling was tedious, but somehow, we would have to make it work.

Six months went by and I became more settled in my new environment. The strangeness of a different home in a new country had transformed into somewhat of an acquaintanceship. I knew that 2 percent milk and orange juice were situated at the periphery of large grocery stores, and I could finally remember how to differentiate between a dime and a nickel. I had discovered how to open a can of evaporated milk and was able to pour it onto my tea without spilling it all over the kitchen counter. I had developed a taste for peanut-butter-and-jelly sandwiches and had become much more self-sufficient than I would have been in Pakistan. I began watching a few basketball games with Phuppa who patiently explained the rules. He was a loyal Lakers fan, and insisted that I did not have much of a choice in the matter, except to become one as well. I still missed the cricket matches, but becoming a Laker's fan was a small sacrifice to win my uncle's confidence.

One morning the phone rang, and it was my mother on the line. She told me that Nana had died in his sleep. I listened to her in shock; he had seemed fine when I had last met him.

"It was his heart," she said, softly.

I had not yet recovered from the loss of my father, and the terrible news of my grandfather's demise was another tragedy I would be mourning for a long time. I felt helpless that I could not hug my mother to get the comfort from her that I needed or give her the reassurance that she needed from me. In a span of three years, she had lost both her parents and her husband.

I was crying, and Phuppo came with a box of tissues and asked me what had happened. She took the phone from me and after offering condolences to my mother, hugged me tightly.

"I loved him so much, Phuppo. I was so mean to him. I didn't even say good-bye properly before I left. I know I hurt him. I was upset with Ammi, really, but I said all my angry words to him instead. And now he's gone. There is nothing I can do to fix what I said."

Phuppo told me that grandparents loved even more than parents did, and they had a special forgiving power. "He is in a great corner of heaven, I'm sure, and looking down at you with pride and joy," she said.

A few months later, Ammi called again. I knew something was different simply by her tone of voice. She did not sound sad, but hesitant, like she had been when she had disclosed her intention to remarry. I wondered what lightening was about to strike me this time. She was telling me about the burglary that happened in the neighborhood and Sahir's new teacher, but I could sense an anxiety in her voice. Finally I asked her, "Why did you call so early in the morning? Is there something important you want to say?"

"Yes, there is, *Beta.* You are going to have another baby brother or sister. I wanted to tell you this great news."

I knew I was supposed to be happy—it would be my brother or sister, after all. But somehow I felt sad and hurt, the idea of my mother moving on with her life, first having a new husband, and now a whole new family. "Congratulations," I muttered, putting the phone down. Would it be my brother or sister? Not really. We would share a mother, but that was all. We had very different fathers. We would not be raised in the same home. Was I really expected to celebrate? Distribute sweets to my relatives on the occasion of this birth? If this were indeed good news for me, my mother would not have hesitated before telling me. She probably knew that it would be another block in the series of hurts that were building inside me, cementing me into an unhappy, angry individual. It would be another crack in our already-crumbling relationship. I could never love that baby. He or she would be my stepfather's child, and that man was my permanent enemy.

The baby was expected on June fourteenth, conveniently during the summer vacation, setting forth the obligation of my presence. I wondered if I would hate the baby as I did my step-father. Hatred was an emotion I had become adept at feeling; it had taken on the role of the extra layer of clothing, a slightly uncomfortable but required companion.

When I greeted my mother, I hugged her and cried, mourn-ing the loss of my grandfather. It was a few days before her due date, and she looked worn out, yet still maintained her elegance. I had taken along some yellow baby clothes that my aunt had helped me pick out. I was not sure which of us had been the more reluctant shopper. Phuppo said that whatever happened, I had to embrace this reality and impart love to my sibling, because, after all, he or she would be innocent and not deserving of anything less.

She was born, a gorgeous baby girl, and we brought her home from the hospital in a light pink dress with white daisies embroidered on it. She was named Sara, in keeping with the tra-dition of *S* names. She was astonishingly beautiful, with pink rosy cheeks and big brown eyes, a true replica of my mother. She would grow up to look just like Ammi, I thought, with strangers being able to decipher their relationship in a crowd. Her room had been decorated in pink and white, and her father seemed like the happiest man in the world. He was not one to smile often, especially not in my presence, and now he was simply glowing with pride. He talked to her as if she could hear and compre-hend every word. To him, she was nothing less than a princess, an angel who had transformed his home into a heaven. I was convinced that now that he had his child and his very own family, we would be reduced to nothing. I worried immensely about Sahir's future.

I was surprised by the warmth I felt toward Sara. Her angelic face immediately melted the resentment I had vowed to feel toward her. I adored her, just like I adored Sahir. I enjoyed helping my mother care for her. I held her and walked the floor at night for hours, singing her softly to sleep. I kept the gripe water handy in case she had a spell of colic. I ran to make her bottle of milk so she would never be hungry. I swaddled her carefully in her blanket so she would always feel warm. She was my only sister and my love for her remained unadulterated by my hatred for her father.

I felt sad when it was time to go back, but I had adjusted to my new life and had no intention of remaining in Pakistan. Everyone including myself had accepted that I was always going to be a visitor in my own home.

On August 17, 1988, the day I was leaving for California, Mr. Rehman summoned everyone to the lounge where the television was on. He said that there was going to be an important announcement. Soon, Ghulam Ishaq Khan was addressing the nation, appearing rather solemn. He announced that the plane carrying President Zia-ul-Haq had crashed. Soon news came that General Zia had indeed died, along with several other passengers, after a ten-year term. Despite the nature of his regime, it was unsettling news, perhaps because he was all that I had known of Pakistan's presidency. It remained unclear what the circumstances of the crash were, and my stepfather was convinced that it was all part of an international conspiracy.

Soon the dormant political parties reemerged with fervor. Bhutto's daughter, Benazir, seemed to be a promising new leader. She was Oxford-educated, dynamic, and an effective speaker, much like her father. She was now the leader of Pakistan People's Party and a candidate for upcoming elections. The other major party was Muslim League, headed by Mian Nawaz Sharif, who also seemed to have a large number of followers. The Muhajir Qaumi Movement, which later came to be known as the Muttahida Qaumi Movement, led by Altaf Hussain, had gained popularity as an important local party in Karachi. It was the voice of the suppressed Muhajirs, the Urdu-speaking community who had migrated from India during the partition days. There appeared to be hope for a new beginning, but that hope was soon dashed when Benazir was elected prime minister and allegations of corruption emerged. I was greatly disappointed, because I had felt a connection with her; she too had lost her father in an extremely tragic way.

Back in California, I talked to Ammi more often to inquire about the baby's progress and what new things she was doing. She had completely stolen everyone's heart, and it seemed as though she had been the missing piece in this now perfect and complete new family. Mr. Rehman had replaced Papa, and Sara had replaced me. Ammi called me less frequently, perhaps because she was consumed by the baby's needs, but to me it felt as though she had a new daughter and no longer needed me in her life.

One night when I was feeling terribly lonely, I called home. Sakina answered and said that everyone had gone out. I stayed up late waiting for a call back, but it never came; perhaps Sakina, who seemed to be getting quite forgetful lately, failed to convey the message. Maybe the twelve-hour time difference had come in to play; it was possible that when they returned they assumed I would be sleeping. To me, however, the most likely explanation was that they had not deemed it necessary to return my call.

Feeling dejected, I went quietly to my aunt's classic music collection, pulled out Barbra Streisand's song "Papa Can You Hear Me," and placed the cassette in my Walkman. I took out some old photographs from my drawer. I had kept them safely with me, but had not had the courage to look at them before.

But now I wanted to make sure that Papa's memory stayed fresh in my mind—the outline of his face, the varying expressions in his eyes. My fear of remembering was being replaced by a newer fear—the fear of forgetting. Would I start forgetting the small details? Was forgetting a part of healing? If it was, then I did not want to heal. I slowly took out the pictures and did not fight the tears that escaped. There was a photograph of my parents' wedding; it was still beautiful, despite having acquired a reddish hue. My mother was dressed in a gorgeous red *gharaara*, appearing like a royal princess, her downcast eyes reflecting her shy demeanor. My father sat beside her in a traditional white *sherwani;* he gazed at her with admiration and with what seemed like a promise to care for her always. Both wore several garlands of fresh red roses.

The next photograph was of the day Sahir had come into this world. Ammi was in a white hospital gown with dark circles under her eyes and an expression of unparalleled joy. I was in the center, my smile showing off a missing tooth, holding Sahir with an ounce of hesitation. Papa had his arms around all of us and looked perfectly content.

There was a picture of all four of us at my ninth birthday: me cutting the black forest cake, Papa helping me blow out the candles, and Ammi holding Sahir. Amna peaking in barely making it into the edge of the photograph. I could not recall what wish I had made that day before extinguishing the candles. Maybe I asked to be first in my class in the upcoming exams. Perhaps I asked for a house for my Barbie doll or a set of mystery Nancy Drew books.

"These are just things," my father had always said. I wished I had asked for my father's long life. I wished I had asked for the well-being and togetherness of my family. I wished I had asked for the preservation of what had been captured in that photograph.

I munched on some chocolate my uncle had bought for me, brushed my teeth, which had been recently freed from braces, and went to bed. I kept replaying the song and fell asleep feeling terribly lonely, with the Walkman in my ears and the words reverberating through my soul:

Papa are you near me?
Papa can you hear me?
The night is so much darker and
The wind is so much colder
The world I see is so much bigger
Now that I'm alone.

Chapter 5

The next four years passed by uneventfully. In 1992, Pakistan brought home the cricket world cup trophy, and the nation found a reason to be proud. The captain, Imran Khan, sounded victorious as he accepted the trophy and announced his plans of opening a high-quality cancer hospital in Lahore in honor of his deceased mother. The win was celebrated across the nation, and a holiday was announced to celebrate. Sahir sounded jubilant on the phone. He told me how he had snuck a radio into school so he and his friends could follow every ball of the nail-biting match.

The balm that time was said to be had slowly begun to heal my sorrow. I missed my father. I missed my homeland. I was in a bigger, cleaner, more opportune, more organized, more scenic part of the world, yet I still missed my country. In the beginning I could not quite define what I missed about Pakistan. Over the years I came to understand that it was a little of everything: our neighbor knocking on the door because she had run out of tomatoes; the fresh guavas sold on the street, the vendors not allowing their enthusiasm to be vanquished by the heat; the Hasina Moin drama that aired from a single channel at eight o'clock at night, mesmerizing the city. I missed the *dhobi* or washman who arrived late each week with all the clothes starched stiff and a towel or two missing from the final count, the grand weddings that were five-day affairs, the *pakoras* fried at the onset of every monsoon, friends chatting and singing to the rhythm of the rain in the balconies of their homes, and most of all, the house full of people and full of voices.

What I missed was a little of everything but a lot of belongingness.

In keeping with the promise I had made to my mother, I spent all my summer vacations in Karachi. Part of me looked forward to it because I craved to feel a connection and I wished for my brother and half-sister to think of me as their older sibling. The person I did not wish to see at all was my stepfather. Time had not healed the wounds or cleared our differences, and my rage remained undiluted. Sara was my dear sister, and I loved her beyond expression. I did feel a pinch when my mother held her close, as it reminded me how her embrace had loosened from around me that dreaded night and had never returned. How I craved a hug, a look of reassurance, and a sense of security from her. It was still difficult to comprehend how the woman who had tended to and nurtured me just as she had her garden had become so alienated from me in such a short time. She had broken my heart by not confiding in me and had put salt on my wounds by replacing my father with a man I could never accept. How she had left her ferns and bougainvilleas in the hands of others in whose care they had failed to thrive. I hoped she would never hurt Sara that way. I was protective of her and loved her with all my heart.

When I left for my summer vacation to Pakistan, I packed everything in a hurry, topping my luggage off with a schoolbag for Zareen, a Nintendo game for Sahir, and a giggling Elmo for Sara. I could not wait to see my baby sister. I knew she would come running to me, and she did. She looked adorable with her hair braided and tied in pink ribbons and her cheeks as rosy as ever. Sahir had glasses and looked leaner than before. Sara was four by then, and had started asking questions which were honest and simple, yet very difficult to answer.

"Why don't you live with us, Apa?" she would ask, her brown eyes wide open. I told her that I was studying in America and maybe when she was older, she could go there as well. I often read to her at night, *Snow White and the Seven Dwarfs* being her favorite, and she asked me to read it to her over and over again. "Mirror, mirror on the wall, who is the fairest of us all?" she would say along with me.

I sang her lullabies until she dozed off to sleep. We named her dolls, braided their hair, and built their imaginary homes. On one occasion we invited all the children from the neighborhood to celebrate a pretend wedding, with the doll wearing fancy clothes that my mother had stitched for her. Sara always looked up to me, searching for the light, trying to imbibe some wisdom; little did she know that the light was actually within her and it was I who wished to absorb the innocence from her. The innocence that had once defined me and had now escaped me, replaced by a coldness that felt numb, yet still painful, like an anesthetic that had not been effective.

One night at the dinner table, she naively remarked, "Abbu, I am going to America with Apa." He looked at her quizzically and shot a harsh glance toward my mother and then toward me. It felt like an accusing arrow piercing through. After Sara was asleep, he came to me and said, "What is this nonsense about Sara going to America?"

Becoming immediately defensive, I replied, "I am sorry if you are offended or threatened, but your daughter asked me why I don't live here and I had to tell her something, so I said it was for my education and she could join me in America if she wished."

"Why should I be threatened? She is not going anywhere. You should have told her the truth—that you don't live here because you ran away and because you were ungrateful."

"Then I would have to tell her why I ran away. It was because of you, and I don't want to spoil your image in her eyes. I would never want a daughter to think badly of her father. She thinks you are perfect."

We went on in this fashion, arguing over nothing, our deep-rooted hatred for each other surfacing in a variety of ways, ruining the peaceful world around us.

"The fact is, I am not perfect, Sana. Nobody is," he said. "But even if I were, for you I would always be the bad guy, the person who took your father's place. You had decided before you even met me that you were going to hate me from the core of your heart. I have come to accept that now, but I think you need to be more considerate of your mother's feelings."

"You don't need to tell me how to handle my mother's feelings; that's between her and me. As for Sara, I love her to death, and if she comes to stay with me for a while, it wouldn't be such a terrible thing. Sahir comes too."

"Sahir has an aunt there. Sara does not. I don't know why we are having this pointless discussion. You don't know how much grief your leaving has caused your mother. Please don't make things more difficult for her."

"My leaving suited you, though. I was the only one talking about my father. When I left, his name left. That's why you never tried to stop me. I am the one who lost everything. For you everything turned out quite well, did it not?"

He looked at me with a disdain I had never seen in his eyes before. As soon as those toxic words escaped my quivering lips, I regretted having said them. But it was too late; the poison had already spread, and the harm had already been done. The damage was unlikely to be reversed by the antidote of an insincere apology. At that instant, I felt the delicate string of the bond between us, loose as it was, break completely.

My stepfather was fuming. I thought he would yell, but instead he crunched his teeth, struggling to control his rage. "I am not going to talk to you anymore. I don't want to say anything that I regret, and I don't want things between your mother and me to become sour. So I will go finish some chores I have pending."

His punishment would come in a discreet and cruel manner. Had he screamed at me, complained to Ammi about me, or beat me with a belt, I would not have felt so much anguish. Instead he tried to keep me away from Sara, taking her with him to the grocery store, finding excuses to put her to bed early. This was my punishment, and in his mind it also benefitted Sara, for he truly believed that I was bad influence on her, which I probably was. She was cute and innocent, and I was stubborn and rebellious. My stepfather had not seen me before the tragedy that had transformed me. I had been just like Sara, more innocent than an unborn child, sweeter than the sweetest sugar. Now I was bitter like the coffee that had been forgotten on the stove and brewed for too long. The worst part was that I did not think I could ever change. By then the well of tears was dry, but the stagnant waters had formed a layer of rust within my soul.

My mother seemed aloof, and I assumed that he had told her something, although I was unable to assess whether he had told her a milder or an exaggerated version of what had taken place. I still did not know him well enough to predict what he would do. I tried my best to avoid all conversation with him, and he did the same. It crossed my mind several times to apologize for my impertinence, but I let my ego kill that thought before acting on it.

I had been told upon my arrival that the schoolbag I had brought for Zareen could be kept in a closet or given away because Sakina had taken her out of school. She was engaged to be married to her cousin, and the boy's family did not want her to be educated beyond eighth grade. I looked sorrowfully at her books, which she had left in a corner of my room, arranged in a neat pile. Perhaps she had not had the courage to throw them away or pack them in her suitcase filled with the dowry her mother had made after taking countless loans from every person she knew.

I spent time with Ammi in the kitchen, which was mostly where she was, engrossed in cooking delicious food and experimenting with new recipes, besides naturally fulfilling her motherly duties with her two other children. I enjoyed watching over Sahir and Sara when the grown-ups were gone and helping Sahir with his homework, although he seldom required it. He aspired to be a doctor, he told me. He said it with a resolve and confidence that was well beyond his nine years. It was pleasant to see glimpses of what a good brother he was to Sara; he played with her, mended all her broken toys, and helped her memorize nursery rhymes. I once heard him singing the *Barney and Friends* theme song to her: "I love you. You love me. We're a happy family."

They were a happy family indeed, but I was not a part of it. I was more like a cousin with a foreign accent from a distant land, living in a different time zone, disconnected with the ups and downs of their everyday lives.

Sahir was a good son to both my mother and stepfather, and I was certain that he did not miss Papa at all. I could not blame him, since he had been too young when the tragedy had occurred. He was growing up with a person he identified as a father figure and was fortunate not to have that piece missing from his life. I realized I had to be happy for him and his situation. Sometimes I felt like telling him everything so he would understand all the reasons behind my departure, but I could not bring myself to break the promise I had made to my mother. Sahir had accepted that Papa was gone for good and that was why Ammi had married the man he called Abbu. Considering how nice he was to Sahir, I sometimes questioned whether my stepfather was as hateful as I believed. But I realized that while Papa continued to live through my memory of him, he was nothing but a hazy childhood dream to Sahir, which was no threat to my stepfather.

Chapter 6

I graduated from high school in 1995. I had been well cared for by my aunt and uncle. They were wonderful parents to me, raising me cautiously and loving me wholeheartedly. I was certain they were more lenient than they would have been if I were their biological child. I attributed that difference to their belief that they had earned all the rights to love me but none to reprimand me. They had given me the best education and life I could have wished for. They were more liberal than my own parents would have been, in that I was permitted to go out with my friends often and make independent decisions. I never stayed out late or did anything to disappoint them, which was my way of expressing my deep gratitude for what they had done for me.

I had always had a passion for writing, and my teachers encouraged me to steer my interests in that direction. I enjoyed reading the newspaper like my dad and spent a considerable amount of time watching CNN. I had decided during my school years that I wanted to become a journalist; I thought it was an occupation that would have made my father proud. The truth had always been so important to him, and a truth seeker is what I wished to be. I shared my thoughts with my aunt, and she agreed that it was definitely a goal worth pursuing, so I diligently set out on that path, never looking back.

I wrote a few articles for the local newspapers and was ecstatic when they were accepted for publication. I had done well in school and had earned a partial scholarship at Stanford. It was an honorable institution that had the advantage of being close to Freemont. Going there was a decision I never regretted. I decided to stay on campus and commuted by the Bart train to my aunt's almost every weekend. Phuppo settled me into an apartment, apprehensive at first about allowing me to live on my own. She discussed the situation at length with my mother over the phone. I knew Phuppo supported me, and I felt deeply obliged. My mother had accepted that I became independent the day I left my abode, and this was not the time to tighten the reigns. Perhaps she was saving that for when the time came for me to get married. When it was all settled, my aunt gave me some cooking lessons and made me promise I would eat well and not allow my books to outweigh me.

"Please don't live off of peanut-butter-and-jelly sandwiches or macaroni and cheese," she said. "The trick with any curry is that you know it's done when the oil comes up above it. If you don't have time to cook chicken curry for yourself, at least boil some lentils and have them with rice."

She packed some pots and pans in a box, along with some spices and recipes. She topped it off with some Nice Biscuits that she had bought from the desi store. She advised me never to run out of salt, sugar, teabags, or turmeric. "You should have some Tylenol in your bedside drawer in case you get sick, and please use sunscreen every day," she added.

We bought some basic furniture and plants and made the apartment look like a place worth coming home to. It was exciting to choose my own furniture and set up everything just as I wanted. The apartment had a small sitting area, a decent-sized bedroom that was large enough to fit in a twin bed and a writing table, and a small but newly finished kitchen. I had chosen it mainly because of the large windows that allowed plenty of sunshine to pour in, creating a bright ambience. It was on the second floor, overlooking a group of towering redwood trees, which appeared fresh despite their senescence. I hung several pictures on the walls and placed a striped brown and beige rug diagonally to give it a contemporary touch.

A part of me looked forward to the independence and the space, but another part of me was frightened of being on my own for the very first time. I knew I was better prepared for an independent college life than I would have been had I been raised back home. I was used to picking up after myself and doing my own laundry. I had at last become accustomed to the quiet and the scarcity of visitors at the door. Nonetheless, I had lived in a very protective environment, had seldom stayed out beyond sunset, and had socialized within a very limited radius. I had been a good student, but now my peers would be among the most competitive, and that added another layer of stress to what I was already feeling. I was skilled at written projects, but oral presentations were my weakness and scared me immensely.

I took the train every weekend and enjoyed the luxury of spending time at what had become my home with those who had become my family. Phuppa was very different from my father; he was less communicative but he was undoubtedly the possessor of a caring heart and was the closest thing I had to a father figure in my life. One day my aunt told me how I had changed him: "He had become so withdrawn over the years. Not having children was hard on me, but it was also hard on him. We had so much love to impart, but no children to give it to. And then you came along like an unexpected parcel at our doorstep and changed everything. You brought back laughter into our lives, Sana."

That was the moment that I realized that even though I had done it subconsciously and unintentionally, without any effort or sacrifice on my part, I had given back a little. Her words helped lift the weight of obligation that I had felt on my shoulders. I also realized that by making a seemingly ridiculous decision at such a young age, I had become the cement holding a marriage together. Had I stayed in Pakistan, I might have become the catalyst tearing a marriage apart.

I was enchanted by Stanford's beauty. Situated in the heart of Palo Alto, it was an architectural masterpiece. I enjoyed walking through the long corridors and letting the warmth of the sunshine touch my face through the intricately designed arches. It was always hot, but the picturesque palm trees that bordered the premises provided a generous shade. Beautiful red and white flowers created a large *S* in the center of the quad. A multitude of students walked and bicycled between classes, and large libraries provided an optimal reading environment. Oak trees that quilted the campus were a reliable cover for unexpected rain. We were told on our orientation day that Stanford's rarely used full name was Leland Stanford Jr. University. It had been named after the Stanfords' teenage son, who had died tragically. I was always intrigued and impressed by people who had the ability to turn grief into something beautiful and honorable, rather than allowing themselves to dissolve in despair.

As I admired the crisp, assiduously cleaned floors, which were a mosaic of gray, white, and brown squares, I sometimes thought of the poor children of Pakistan who sat on the dusty ground, starving and sweating in the heat, fervently memorizing their lessons. I wondered how many of them never went to school, and questioned how many, like Zareen, had their education interrupted suddenly because their parents did not have the means or the will to let them pursue their dreams. A large number of them were possibly so bright, they could outshine the best graduate of Stanford. I was blessed to be studying what I wanted to at one of the world's most prestigious schools. I had worked hard to be where I was but had also been very fortunate.

Many of my earlier courses focused on language and literature, and my assignments often involved reading and reviewing books, which had been my long-standing passion. I always tried to remember Professor Davis's words, "When you write, make the product unforgettable. If you have had any setbacks in life, remember that they are your greatest assets. If you have sadness inside you, write with your tears. If you have anger raging in you, use it as your weapon."

I loved to write but continued to dread presentations. For days beforehand, I would pray that my anxiety would not show through and that my voice would remain steady as I spoke. I always lost points on my speeches and struggled to maintain a satisfactory grade point average. I once had to give a talk on the assigned topic of "The Pleasures and Perils of Technology," which I spent weeks preparing for. I edited it several times after the first draft and rehearsed it countless times before the day of the presentation, placing extra teabags in my mug to help me stay awake through the night. I shook as I walked toward the podium, and by the time I reached it, I forgot all the words. I looked at the paper copy I had in my hand, took a deep breath, and started,

"Here at Stanford, we are amidst the best technological minds in the world. I believe that technology begins with an idea, which is its birth, and then advances over time with better ideas and innovations, which are not its death, but its reincarnation."

I struggled to continue, but my voice shook and I felt light-headed. Suddenly my mouth became so dry that I started coughing and nearly choked. A thoughtful colleague quickly brought me a glass of water. After thanking her, I attempted to resume my speech, but time was running out, and I did not know which parts to skip and which to include in my disastrous speech.

"...Paradox of lost communication between people by devices meant for improving communication..."

I was stuttering and could not stop my hands from shaking uncontrollably. I suddenly lost my train of thought and stopped in the midst of a sentence, unable to find my voice. Embarrassed, I stepped down, mumbling a general apology and wondering if I would have to repeat the semester. I was tearful, miserable, and felt defeated beyond expression. My professors were of the opinion that this degree of stage fright and lack of confidence was sure to hinder my success and suggested that I meet with a counselor. They were willing to work with me and give me some time, and I was eternally grateful for that.

That evening I talked to my aunt, narrating to her an abridged version of my disastrous afternoon. She consoled me, as she always did, and offered encouragement. For the remainder of the evening, I curled up on my couch, trying in vain to cheer myself up with an episode of *Everybody Loves Raymond* while devouring the leftover Halloween candy from the month before.

Despite my struggles with confidence, I soon became well integrated and adjusted in Stanford's congenial environment. I had two good friends: Jennifer, who had been with me since middle school, and Kavita, whom I had met in college. Jennifer was a student of architecture, and Kavita was majoring in psychology. Jennifer's parents had been divorced since we had been in school, and she had grown up without her father, who had remarried and relocated to Michigan soon after the divorce. She frequently used her good sense of humor to dilute her problems, and it often helped me put mine on the back burner as well. She had blue eyes and long, blonde hair and was constantly entertaining us with her collection of memorized blonde jokes. I remember how we all laughed when she told us the one about the blonde and the brunette betting on a newscast: "So a blonde and a brunette were watching the six o'clock news, which included a report of a man threatening to jump off the San Francisco Bridge. The blonde bet her brunette friend hundred dollars that he wouldn't jump. He jumped, so the blonde gave her friend fifty dollars. The brunette confessed that she had already seen the footage on the five o'clock news, so she really couldn't take the money. 'So did I,' said the blonde. 'But I didn't think he would jump again.'"

Kavita was from Bombay, India. She had dark skin and sharp features, which were complemented by thick black hair that she wore in a bob cut. She was sweet and down-to-earth, and although she had the blessing of both parents, she had lost her eight-year-old sister to typhoid. Tragedy had brought us all together and wrapped us in a tight blanket of friendship, protecting us from the harsh winters of our troubled memories.

Jennifer and Kavita were both more open than I was and did not have much trouble expressing their feelings. We all knew how to laugh at ourselves, so I would share jokes about Pakistanis, and Kavita would come up with jokes about Indians. Kavita and I would often indulge in Desi talk, much to Jennifer's chagrin. I would ask Kavita all about the Indian movie stars and the latest Bollywood gossip. We would sing songs often, from the oldies from the sixties, to the latest ones from the nineties, and Jennifer would be amused by our repertoire of memorized lyrics. She was astonished when she heard stories of people having arranged marriages. Kavita was already engaged to her aunt's husband's nephew and seemed content with the matrimony planned for a few years later.

One day Jennifer, after having an argument with her father over the phone, called me to share her pain. I had just spoken to my stepfather and was also feeling down. He had had an appendectomy, and my mother insisted that I inquire after his health.

"Let's go out and try to feel better," Jennifer suggested. When I agreed, she said we should go to the bar for a drink.

"No, Jennifer. You know I don't drink, and I won't let you do it either; I don't want you to get hurt."

"Oh, please. Do you think our parents care? If they don't, then why should we? Stop preaching and come with me."

She kept insisting that I join her and promised it would make me feel better. I told her that I could not do something that was forbidden to me by my religion. I was not very pious—I had missed several prayers and fasts and I had not been an obedient daughter—but I could not consume alcohol. I had no attraction to something that claimed seventy thousand lives each year in this country alone, that changed a person in every way.

"Even if it makes you happy, how long does that happiness last?" I said, trying to convince her.

"Well, the happiness after watching a good movie, listening to a good song, reading a good book, or eating a delicious meal doesn't last either. That's why we find happiness in small packages and combine them together to create true happiness."

"Actually a really good book and a really good song can give you lasting happiness, or at least they can stay with you a long time and help you grow. Music and literature make this world a better place and they certainly do not take your senses away from you. They don't make you do things you would otherwise never consider doing. They don't change who you are."

We continued to argue until I realized that I was not going to succeed in changing her mind. "If you aren't going to listen, I'll come with you, but only to drive you back home. I'll wait outside."

So that was what we did. From that day on, we both accepted that we could not change each other, but that did not mean we could not still be friends. I had perhaps always been overly judgmental with Jennifer, not realizing that I was subconsciously terrified of outside influences swaying me from who I was. By then I was older and past my unsure teenage years. My vision had become sharper, and I realized that differences between our religion, culture, and upbringing would not cease to exist or stop coloring the disparate decisions we made in our lives. But rather than perceiving these differences as barriers, I started looking at them as photographs of the same building taken from different angles, each capturing a unique beauty and, when put side by side, each complementing the other, adding a third dimension to an otherwise two-dimensional composition.

Chapter 7

My father had been taken from me because of his death. My mother and brother had been taken from me because of my mother's marriage, which I still had not accepted. Sahir would come to visit during holidays, and I would go in the summers, but there was still a cold war between my stepfather and me, partly to be blamed on his ego, and perhaps equally to be blamed on my obstinacy. Ammi tried to be part of my life, but I did not make much of an effort to include her. I had not been able to forgive her yet. I could not attach any blame to my brother, and whenever I looked at him, I wondered how wonderful it would have been to share my life with my only full sibling. At every visit, I felt the gap between us becoming more and more substantial. The separation between my family and I, as well as my country and I.

I felt my motherland's embrace loosen from around me, as I had my mother's nine years earlier. When I visited, I became less tolerant of the power outages and mosquito bites that I had grown up with. It saddened me deeply to see young children begging on the streets or being used for cheap labor. The large, extravagant weddings in a country riddled with poverty seemed surreal. Distance had given me perspective, the ability to judge as an outsider, but it had robbed me of the unconditional element of the love I had previously felt.

In Karachi, when I was in the car, I felt as if the trucks and buses were within millimeters of me and I marveled at the courage of all the drivers who managed to reach their destination without incident. I coughed each time I breathed in the smoke escaping the yellow mini buses, as if my lungs had lost the strength to inhale this previously familiar air. I enjoyed the fragrance carried by the evening breeze, of the fresh roses and the white *chamelis* being sold at the roadside, yet I would brace myself for the stench of fish emanating from the trucks that followed. I never stopped enjoying the tasty meals, yet I would always get ill with gastroenteritis, as if the same food and water I had consumed for years had become alien to me, less forgiving because I had left. I had changed from player to spectator, from actor to an inattentive member of the audience, from a tree of the soil to a plant that was growing in another garden and no longer belonged to that same part of the Earth. Like the immune system rejecting a donated organ or an expression of poetry lost in translation: this was my redefined relationship with my homeland as well as with my family.

During one of my visits, Sara sat down next to me after we had all finished taking down the decorations for her eighth birthday party. "What was your father like?" she asked. It was a simple, straightforward question, but it was completely unexpected. The answer could have been given in volumes. What my father was like was the thought that had consumed my life—what he had been like and what he would have been like had fate not snatched him away from me. My father had been a personification of honesty and integrity. He had been a symbol of humility. He had been the foundation on which our family had stood, the glue that had kept us all together. He had been funny and lively and forever putting others before himself. But I did not know what to say to Sara just then. I had never discussed with her that she was not my real sister, and Ammi and Sahir had not prepared me for this confrontation.

My strained relationship with my stepfather had undoubtedly raised questions in her intelligent mind, and she had asked them in a manner that was both simple and forthright, Sahir later told me. She was old enough and mature enough to understand

and accept that Sahir and myself were her half siblings and that her parents had been married to other people before. She was perturbed for a day or two but then gracefully accepted that new revelation as a minor wrinkle in her otherwise well-ironed life.

"He was the best father in the world," I finally said, summing up all my thoughts and at last finding the strength to verbalize them.

"Tell me more about him," she said,

"I suppose it's strange to talk to Ammi about him, and Abbu never met him, and Sahir doesn't remember much."

In my home where my brother and mother never mentioned his name, my half sister was asking me about him; my half sister, who had no relationship with him and who would not have come into this world had he been alive.

"Would you like to see a picture?" I said, and she nodded. I pulled out the wallet-size version of the family portrait from my purse. She paused for a moment and then said, "Wow, you look just like him." I asked her if she would like to keep it, and she said she would. I wrote her name on the back of it and made her promise to keep it in a secret place where her father would not be able to find it.

We chatted into the early hours of the morning about my father, her father, and the complexities of human relationships. We talked about our maternal grandparents, whom she had never seen.

"You got your nose from Nana, as well as your love for cookies," I said. "And I inherited his love for chocolate, as well as his passion for reading." My mother and stepfather were exhausted from having hosted the party, so they had gone to bed early, and Sahir took his leave to devote himself to his books. He was constantly studying, even during vacations. He had vowed to ace all his exams in order to fulfill his dream of going to medical school.

Sara told me that she loved me just the same, and it did not matter to her that we had different fathers. She told me she had never really believed the fallacy that I had left for a better education. It did bother her that I had left and that I did not get along with her father. Mature as she was, however, she said that if she were in my shoes, she would probably react in the same way. I was proud of my thoughtful sister, who, even at that tender age, had the ability to be so nonjudgmental.

Even though my stepfather had kept me away from Sara and had never encouraged her to call me on her own or spend too much individual time with me, it was comforting to know that he had at least not attempted to influence her opinion of me or sabotage our sisterhood. For the first time in my life, in my heart, I gave him some credit.

I had barely returned from my summer vacation, when, on September 20, 1996, Sahir called and said there had been terrible shooting close to where our home was. He said it was loud and had gone on for several hours. The next morning news came that the shooting had been at Bilawal House and Benazir's brother, Murtaza Bhutto, who had also been politically inclined, had been killed. Apparently there had been almost one hundred policemen hiding around the house and inside the trees, and they had shot Murtaza along with his friend. He had been left to bleed for forty-five minutes and had died there. All the while his wife and daughter had been inside the house, listening to the shooting. That murder joined the unfortunately long list of crimes that had gone unpunished. Years later, Murtaza's daughter Fatima Bhutto shared her conviction that this execution did not occur without the knowledge of her father's sister Benazir, and Benazir's husband Asif Ali Zardari. Zardari had by then acquired fame as "Mr. Ten Percent," a nickname that alluded to the unlawful profits he had made on several national and international deals. Regardless of what the reason was behind this assassination, my heart went out to Fatima Bhutto, who had lost her father to murder at the age of fourteen.

Sahir visited the following winter. He had turned out a fine young boy who would have made our papa proud. He had started looking a lot like him and had the same kind voice, generous smile, and confident stride.

"I think you should give our stepfather another chance, Apa," he said. "He is really a nice person. I wish you could have known him better. He has given me as much love as he has given Sara. He would have given it to you too, if only you had let him."

"So tell me about the pretty girls in your school," I said, changing the subject. "Will Maryam graduate with you? Does she want to go into medicine too? She was so cute as a little girl; she must have grown up to be really beautiful."

"Come on, Apa," he said shyly, exasperated at my resolve to avoid all conversation about my stepfather. "I know you keep avoiding this subject, but your defiance has created a lot of problems. You are my older sister, so I have never been able to tell you this, but I cannot stand it that you don't have a relationship with our father. It really bothers me, and you never try."

"Sahir, firstly he is not our father; our father died many years ago. Secondly, I cannot understand why you always side with him, when I'm the one who's your flesh and blood," I said, my tone revealing my irritation.

"For me, he is as good a father as I could have. He is the one who taught me how to ride a bike; he is the one who bandaged my knee when I fell off that same bike, when my sister, my flesh and blood, could have done all of that but wasn't there. I wanted to be able to cherish memories of Papa, and you don't know how hard it has been for me to have everything so vague in my memory. You were the only one who could have helped me remember, but before I knew it, you were gone."

Sahir had never complained to me in this way, and I was angry that my baby brother, whom I had taught how to speak, was now talking back to me. Unable to keep my voice down any longer, I said, "How could you? You think I was happy to leave?"

"Maybe you weren't happy, but no one forced you. It was your own idea, your own choice. Life is full of choices, Apa. Papa's passing was not your choice, but your leaving was."

I was hurt, angry, and helpless. If I told him everything, maybe he would understand the extent of my devastation and forgive me for having left him. "You don't know how it was for me," I said, sitting back and forcing myself to appear calm while deciding against continuing the story.

That night I pulled out a slab of chocolate that had been sitting in the refrigerator and bit on it slowly, hoping that it would obliterate the bad taste in my mouth. I was surprised that Sahir had harbored all these emotions for so long. While his words wounded me, I was relieved to think that at least I had been missed, even if it meant that I had been blamed.

Chapter 8

It was February 11, 1997, ten years exactly since the worst day of my life. Professor Reynolds's creative writing class had been cancelled because he had called in sick. I was doing well in college, despite the oral presentations and was consumed by papers to submit and assignments to complete. Exams that always seemed too close. Time that never seemed enough.

My higher education had given me a new focus. I carried with me the burden of my past, but I thought of college as a fresh, interesting, and partially read chapter in the story of my life. I enjoyed spending time with Jennifer and Kavita, and I was content—not happy, but content. Happiness still seemed like an unattainable goal, an unreachable star in a vast sky. I laughed with my friends and counted my blessings every day, but my father's death and the daunting image of his ruthless killer were always on my mind. I thought of seeking counseling on campus but always managed to find excuses not to.

Disappointed that my favorite class had been cancelled and unable to ignore the date, I walked slowly toward an unknown destination. I felt as though I was walking with a visible robe of gloom draped across my shoulders. I considered returning to my apartment for a few hours, but that would have meant having to rush back for the next class. I had already spoken to my mother, brother, and Phuppo earlier that morning. Kavita was in India, and Jennifer was completely immersed in her project of drawing the Twin Towers from four different angles. I began walking toward the library, thinking I would complete my character sketch of *Elizabeth Bennett* from *Pride and Prejudice,* but then I decided to simply sit in the peaceful courtyard beside the chapel and remember Papa for a while.

For the last ten years, I had made it a point to spend some time in silence on the anniversary of his death. It had been so long, but the pain still felt excruciating, like a wound that was fresh and eons away from healing. It was a reminder of the loss, a preparation for another year without Papa's presence. I was sitting quietly on one of the benches and reminiscing when I noticed a young man seated on the bench across from me. He was strikingly handsome and seemed immersed in deep thought. He was holding a thick brown book, but it was obvious that he was not reading it. From his appearance, I guessed he was Desi.

I was never one to initiate a conversation but somehow that day I mustered the courage to speak. I did not want to appear too forward and I certainly did not wish to trespass on his reverie. Perhaps he had a test and was memorizing something in this peaceful corner or was revising a presentation in his head. It might be unpleasant and inappropriate to disturb him. Yet I could not shake off the deep inclination to talk to him. I was intrigued by his complete obliviousness to my presence and presumed he was thinking about a serious subject.

From the corner of my eye, I saw a bright orange butterfly pause for a few seconds before soaring into the sky above.

"Are you missing somebody?" I asked, shocked to hear myself say the words.

Startled, he looked up, and his thoughtful face softened into an endearing smile. "Yes. In fact, I was. You are quite a mind reader. Now that I have answered your question, may I inquire whether you are enjoying *Pride and Prejudice?*"

"Yes. I'm doing a book review project on it."

"What did you learn about Pride and what did you learn about Prejudice?" He maintained a serious yet inquisitive expression while posing the question. I thought for a moment and answered,

"I guess that pride takes away one's ability to speak, and prejudice deprives one of the ability to see."

Feeling a sudden surge of sadness creep over me, I looked down at the ground. I had just realized that the time I had spent without my father had become greater than the time I had spent with him. "I was missing somebody too," I said, not sure if our conversation should end there. He had come a little closer, and I could see the silhouette of our shadows on the ground. "But it's not what you think," I continued. "I'm not upset about a broken relationship, the common theme for sorrow among college students." The bright rays of the sun made me squint, and I was grateful to find an excuse to look at the ground once again.

"No, I didn't assume that at all," he replied reassuringly. "I try to stay away from pride as well as prejudice. I just hope that whoever you are missing can come back."

I briefly looked up at his eyes, immediately sensing warmth in them. "No, unfortunately not," I said solemnly.

"Then we have something in common. I was missing my mother. She died eight years ago, when I was thirteen. I miss her and sometimes come here to talk to her."

We had just met, and he was already sharing with me the personal and poignant details of his life. This was in sharp contrast to me. It had taken me years to share the tragedy of my childhood with even those I considered to be my closest friends.

"I'm so sorry for your loss," I said. "It was my father I was mourning. I lost him a long time ago too, when I was nine, but it still hurts."

This was a very unusual beginning to a friendship. We continued to talk, and before I knew it, several hours had passed. I missed my literature class for the very first time but felt relieved after having opened my heart to someone who had been eager to listen.

His name was Ahmer, and he too was from Pakistan, as I had suspected. His hair was dark and fell casually on his forehead. His eyes were almost black and were intense, as if they were holding layer upon layer of thought and concealing volumes of pain. But they were also kind and caring, as if they could soak up and eradicate another's agony. He had a dimple in his chin that became more pronounced as he smiled. A subtle scar from a childhood mishap, perhaps, ran across his right cheekbone. He was a law student and had dreamed of becoming a lawyer since his teenage years. Both his parents had left this world. The more recent loss had been that of his mother, who had lost her battle with breast cancer at the age of thirty-six. He had been subsequently cared for by his maternal aunt.

We discussed the political and economic problems Pakistan continued to face, the changes in the cricket team, and the mouthwatering *seekh kababs* at Barbecue Tonight. We talked about the sands of Clifton Beach and the cool Karachi breeze. I told him how I loved to pick up the beautiful seashells that washed up on shore. We talked about how Hasina Moin's plays made us laugh and cry and how Noor Jehan's songs touched our hearts. We shared a love for old and new Indian and Pakistani songs and soon agreed to share each other's collections.

"I remember I was constantly in a rush to complete my homework so I could make it in time for the team selection of the cricket being played in my street," he said. "The best was when they put streetlights on our road, so we could have night matches. We all went crazy when Pakistan won the world cup in 1992."

"Who could forget that?" I said, "I wasn't there, but my brother said they kept listening to the commentary on the radio in their classrooms and after we won, a national school holiday was announced to celebrate. That's how important cricket is. I saw Imran Khan holding the world cup trophy when I watched the recorded footage that my brother had saved."

"Imran Khan went beyond cricket when he formed the cancer hospital in his mother's name. Naturally I feel a kinship with him for that and I have hope that the political party he began last year will bring some good."

"I heard the party is called Tehreek-e-Insaaf."

"Yes. It's new, but at least it means 'movement for justice.' If they can bring about justice, I will support them."

"I'm so out of touch with cricket now, I don't even know the names of the new players."

"Yeah, it's hard to keep up. I've tried to love basketball and football, and the teams at Stanford are great, but I just haven't been able to get used to the feel. I'm no good at baseball because I keep holding the bat like a cricket bat." He went on, "When I left Pakistan, I left a part of me behind, and the moment I stepped foot in America, I took a part of it and made it mine. Once you leave your country, you are always regarded by your people as a foreigner, and the country you migrate to regards you as the same. So I guess I always feel like a foreigner, even though I love both my countries."

"I know what you mean," I replied. "It's like you're always pulling at your mother country's apron strings, and the pull is far away, but it's a strong one. With time you grow up, and the pull starts to loosen a bit, but the bond remains strong. The greatest challenge is blending in while never forgetting who you are."

Ahmer nodded in agreement and said, "My relationship with my homeland is somewhat like a marriage; initially you turn a blind eye to your spouse's faults, then you try to fix them, and eventually you learn to accept them and love them because they make the person who they are. The streets of Karachi would not be the same if water didn't flood them every monsoon, and the roadside fruit *chaat* would lose its charm if it were served in a detergent-washed bowl in an upscale restaurant."

"It's hard sometimes not to think about the good old times, the carefree days," I said. "But whenever I go back to Pakistan, it is usually a rude awakening; I'm reminded that it's no longer the Pakistan of my childhood. It's hard to believe that Karachi has enjoyed the title of 'City of Lights.' Sitting with you here today, I'm getting nostalgic talking about these things with you. All those little ordinary things we mentioned—the guavas, the mangoes, the fresh pastries from the roadside bakery, and the bazaars overflowing with crowds the night before Eid—the ordinary things that made life extraordinary."

I enjoyed Ahmer's company so thoroughly that minutes turned into hours, as words poured like a waterfall. Not once did I, the introverted girl that I was, pause to think before speaking. Not once did either of us look at our watches. Not once did I feel a twinge of guilt for having missed my literature class for the very first time. I had not felt such genuine happiness in years. And that was despite the palpable sadness of my father's tenth death anniversary.

Chapter 9

Our friendship grew strong very quickly. It blossomed parallel to the purple jacarandas in the quad signaling the bloom of spring. We laughed, listened to music, and often had lunch together. We usually ate on campus but sometimes ventured into nearby eateries, mostly the Chinese restaurant Jing-Jing. We would chat about our days in college over the sizzle of barbecued shrimp and share our childhood over the aroma of hot and sour soup. Life seemed to be turning into a sweet alley, even though it might have been a blind one, and I was losing the need to fill it up needlessly with chocolate.

Jennifer and Kavita started teasing me long before I had confessed to them what I had in my heart. Jennifer would say, "There's a bounce in your step, my dear," and

"I've known you for so many years and have never seen you smile or laugh so much. Whatever this source of your happiness is, may it last a lifetime. I can't wait to hear about it."

Kavita would say, "What's up with you? Your singing has improved tremendously. You are hitting the high notes effortlessly. You are far more in tune than I am, and I spent four years learning classical music. I can tell what it is: you are singing all those romantic songs with your heart, as if you are thinking about someone."

They were constantly upset that I no longer had time for them and was always making excuses, saying I had tests to prepare for and assignments to submit. "You are awfully busy for the beginning of the semester," Jennifer would mumble, not believing my story.

When I was ready to share my secret, I had my friends over for dinner. I waited for Jennifer to narrate her blonde joke of the evening.

"OK, so she goes to get a haircut and tells the hairdresser not to take off the headphones she's wearing or she'll die," she said in her usual animated tone. "But the hairdresser forgets and takes them off. Soon after, the blonde has a pretty haircut, but she's lying there dead. Nobody can understand what happened, and then they find her headphones and listen to the taped recording. It says, 'Breathe in, breathe out. Breathe in, breathe out.'"

We had a good laugh and started devouring the roasted chicken. As we ate, I casually informed them that I had something important to share. "I met someone," I said.

Jennifer let the fork in her hand drop. "I knew it! I knew you were up to something. That radiance doesn't just show up on someone's face without a really good reason," she said, jumping out of her chair. She came over to me and gave me a tight hug.

"Who is he?" asked Kavita, reaching over to be included in the hug. "We want details!"

I was suddenly inundated with their questions: "What's his name? How old is he? Where is he from? When did you meet him? When can we meet him?"

"Let me get some dessert," I said, trying to escape for a few minutes and not knowing quite where to start.

"Come on, Sana," Kavita argued, "You know you don't have to serve us. We will help ourselves. We practically hang out here all the time."

"Yeah," said Jennifer. "It's more fun at your place, although you guys are welcome to hang out more often at mine, but you won't be able to find anything unless you can swim through the mess."

"That's not true, Jennifer," I remarked. "You are pretty neat, just not when your assignments are due. But even then, there are pencils and stencils everywhere. At least there is a method to your madness."

I proceeded to tell them how Ahmer and I had met and how in sync we seemed to be. We were just friends, I told them; I did not know how he felt about me and certainly was not planning to ask. I told them how perfect I thought he was for me, and we spent the next few hours chatting and laughing uncontrollably.

Jennifer helped me hang up one of her sketches that I had asked her for, my favorite angle of the Twin Towers that she had made for her project. It was an oblique view of the World Trade Center towering above the rest of the Manhattan skyline in the early hours of the morning. It was commendable how she had replicated the impression of height on a sixteen-by-twenty canvas so well. We placed it next to her other two drawings that covered my wall. This arrangement had worked out well, it had helped decorate my sitting room with meaningful art, and assisted Jennifer in finding a good home for her dear paintings, which would otherwise have collected layers of dust in her apartment. I had moved all the photographs into my bedroom, including my very treasured family portrait, and had turned the lounge into what I called "Jennifer's gallery." One of the paintings depicted Shah Faisal Mosque in Islamabad, an architectural asset of Pakistan. I had given Jennifer a photograph of it, and she had drawn the tall minarets surrounding the tent-shaped center on the backdrop of the scenic Margalla hills. She had submitted it for an assignment about The Modern Architecture of Southeast Asia. The third was a pen drawing of the Stanford quad, with its intricately constructed arches and the shadows they cast, and included a couple of students in the midst of a busy day. I admired it and knew it would forever be my valued possession, as it was a beautiful depiction of my alma mater. But now, after having met Ahmer there, that artistic sketch had acquired a new meaning for me altogether.

Over the next few months, I continued to talk to Ahmer and liked everything I learned about him. I had subtly made it clear to him that I was from a conservative, traditional family, and the only step beyond a platonic friendship that I would consider would be marriage, which would have to occur through the proper channel, after a proposal to my family. We only talked about these things indirectly.

There was a mystery about him that I found intriguing, and I was not in any hurry to unravel it. He would sometimes get a faraway look in his eyes, but it would be gone before I had a chance to read it. He seemed to have a magnetic force emanating from him that was gradually pulling me out of my cocoon. I thought briefly about the comparison he had drawn about his relationship with Pakistan being like a marriage. It was unusual for a single person to be so insightful about the complications of marriage, but then he was an unusual, multifaceted person and seemed to know a lot about everything. I smiled to myself, thinking his understanding about married life may come in handy later.

In the summer, I finally gave in to the pressure from my friends and introduced him to Jennifer and Kavita. To my delight, they liked him tremendously.

"He's cool," Jennifer had said. "I really like him, and I'm not saying that just to flatter you."

"He seems like a guy with a backbone, and forgive the cliché, but a tall, dark, and handsome one at that. Plus I think you both look great together," Kavita commented.

I was pleased that my friends had approved of him. They were honest, and I knew they had set the bar high for me and were undoubtedly in a position to be far more objective than myself. Their opinion mattered and helped me seal my trust in my own sentiments.

I met his friends too, a group of girls and boys who all seemed quite amiable; we would often go out as a group to eat or occasionally to watch a movie. My one-to-one conversation with Ahmer was mostly on the phone or chatting on the computer. Occasionally we would meet on campus or have lunch together.

"Abida Parveen is coming to San Francisco," Ahmer told me one day, referring to a famous Pakistani singer. "You want to go to her show?" he asked casually.

"Sure, I'd love to. My father loved her *ghazals*, and I've heard a few. I'll ask Kavita if she wants to go," I said nervously, thinking it was imperative to have her come along.

"Yes, sure," he replied, trying to conceal his disappointment that I would not be his sole companion. "Let me know soon, because I hear the tickets are selling fast."

We went, and Ahmer insisted he pay for everyone's tickets. I wore my new purple *shalwar kameez* that Ammi had sent a month before. I changed my lipstick three times to ensure that it was the right shade and applied the mascara that had been sitting untouched for months in the top drawer of my dressing table. I wore my new black shoes and wondered how uncomfortable the long walk from the parking garage to the auditorium was going to be in the high heels I was so unaccustomed to wearing.

If I was willing to sacrifice my comfort for my appearance, I was certainly starting to care how I looked. The week before I had dropped off an enormous carton at Goodwill that was filled to the brim with my worn jeans, slacks, and gray sweatshirts, the latter of which Jennifer had been convincing me to get rid of for the last year. I had gone shopping with Kavita, treating myself to the new pair of stylish black shoes. I was never one to shop, as I seldom felt the need or saw the point of indulging in such extravagance. I had remembered what my father said about material things—that they could never be a source of lasting joy. I was always mindful of the hard-earned money my aunt and uncle sent me. I insisted that my mother not send me anything beyond my college tuition, which was partly covered by what I had inherited from my father; the remainder was being paid for by my stepfather. His financial contribution to my education continued to bother me at several levels. It made my improper attitude toward him seem less justifiable and the "ungrateful" label appear more befitting. But that day, I selected the exquisite pair of shoes without once looking at the price tag or rummaging through the clearance rack.

I stood before my recently bought full-length mirror, pushed my hair back one last time, rearranged my *dupatta* so it fell gracefully over my shoulders, and felt sure that this was the longest I had ever spent getting ready for something—or someone. It was a wonderful, memorable night. Abida's talent for enticing the audience with her beautiful poetic songs was unlike anything I had heard before. I knew Sahir would be envious when I told him. I would skip out the details of who accompanied me, of course. Ahmer softly whispered to me that I looked fantastic. "Traditional clothes really suit you; you should wear them more often." I was grateful for the darkness in the auditorium that hid the scarlet rising in my cheeks.

Abida Parveen continued to sing Parveen Shakir's beautiful words:

The word of our love spread in every corner,
My beloved welcomed me just like a fragrance.
May your surroundings as well as your heart always be
filled with joy,
May you never face the calamity of the eve of loneliness.

I had a presentation the following morning, and Ahmer, who had been working on healing me of my stage fright, felt that it was ideal to relax the night before, rather than memorizing and rehearsing countless times. He told me the trick was to have everything prepared at least two weeks in advance and then practice it a few times every day.

"The last week, just think of it as something that has become second nature, and the day before, don't even look at it. Get a good night's sleep, have a cup of coffee or tea in the morning, and be ready to go. Dress well, look confident, and be yourself."

I told him these were all great tips, but what was I supposed to do when I got up there? Facing and addressing the audience was the hardest part for me. He told me to remember one thing: "You may not know everything about everything, but what you are going to discuss you know the best. You have researched it and you have learned it, so nobody in the audience can beat you. Your goal is to make sure no one falls asleep. If the content is good, which I'm sure it always is, and you speak in slightly varying tones, you are guaranteed to keep everyone awake. If you can punctuate it with some humor, that's even better, but start doing that later, once you've mastered the confidence part. Another trick is to pretend you are the only one in the room, but the problem with that one is you don't connect well with the audience. But nowadays you can because of the whole PowerPoint thing. It's dark in the room, so no one can really see you; you just have to ensure that the confidence shows through your voice. Talk slowly so everything seems well thought out. Talk clearly so you that you can be heard. Don't be too soft, but don't be too loud either, because if what you say is sensible and true, it will be heard without screaming it out."

"You are so right, Ahmer. These are all great suggestions. I just hope I can get over this fear. What do I do at the end? I'm always scared of getting bombarded with questions, and there are many points to gain or lose in the question-and-answer session."

"It helps to summarize your talk at the end. Then ask the audience if they have any questions you can answer. They are going to ask questions anyway, and if you set the stage for that in advance, it makes you appear more confident. Just remember that if there are questions and if you have sparked a debate, that's great. That means they were listening and they care enough to require clarification. Let the questions become your booster rather than your intimidator. Try to predict beforehand what questions can be asked. You can practice in front of someone else and see what questions they come up with. Answer as best as you can, and don't get overwhelmed."

I followed Ahmer's advice to the fullest, and it worked like magic. I could not believe how well I did the next morning. The speech was titled "America's Political Achievements and Mistakes." My heart raced as I walked through the corridors into the presentation room, but my hands did not shake and my voice did not tremble. I walked in as the new, confident me. I had it memorized on my fingertips and I had read around it, after having rehearsed it before Ahmer, and once in front of Kavita. I felt adequately prepared to field questions, especially those around the Vietnam War.

For the first time, giving a speech was almost enjoyable, rather than being the burdensome chore it once was. I was conscious of the fact that everyone noticed the transformation I had undergone. Afterwards, Professor Davis caught up with me and said that I had earned an A for my presentation. I was ecstatic and ran across the arched corridor with a wide grin on my face, letting the golden sunlight pour generously on my face, permitting the wind to tangle the strands of my hair. I jumped on the squares on the floor, stones that each graduating class had placed since the opening of Stanford in 1891. I raced like a child who had just mastered the art of running, leaping onto each stone: 1995, 1996, 1997. I had taken a semester off initially when I had been overwhelmed, and there were some moments that had raised doubts in my mind about my future. But I had come a long way, and I knew that there would be many more inscriptions, and there would be one for 2001. And for the first time, I felt confident that I would be part of that stone.

I told Ahmer I owed it all to him, and he modestly replied, "It was you up there, Sana, not me. You have every reason to be confident. I am proud of you."

From that day on, I started enjoying presentations, and they soon became my strength rather than my weakness. I volunteered for the topics that were left unselected and signed up to intern at a local news channel. Was this really me? The hand shaking, voice trembling, timid girl who had feared the audience worse than a head on collision? I could not believe that I was taking on the challenge of facing thousands of people and actually looking forward to it.

Ahmer had changed me in so many ways that I did not feel like the same person. I felt prettier, taller. I felt much happier than before. My life seemed to be unfolding like the undulating notes of a symphony in the midst of a beautiful composition. I enjoyed my internship thoroughly and finalized my decision to pursue a career in broadcasting. It gave me a great appreciation of all the hard work behind the scenes. I learnt that the one-hour newscast was much more than that one-hour, that in fact, it involved a full day of preparation.

One evening, as we were sitting in the quad after another day of hard work, Ahmer showed me a picture of his mother, a young lady in her thirties with a radiant smile and thick, glossy black hair.

"She was beautiful," I said, a sadness overcoming me as I realized I would never know this woman, who had raised her son so well. "You have her eyes, Ahmer, and her hair was so becoming, so shiny."

"Yes. She had gorgeous long hair. She would brush it with a special brush and put coconut oil and henna in it. And then the chemotherapy made it all come out. She was a really strong woman who went through a lot of physical and emotional pain and never showed it. But the night her hair came out, she cried for hours, and so did I."

"I'm sorry," I said, feeling his pain and wanting to share it, and hoping to dampen it with words of comfort that I could not find. I had always thought that my pain had been so intense because my father had died so suddenly, leaving me no time to prepare for it. But when I thought of Ahmer's pain, it did not seem any less, because he had seen his mother dying slowly and painfully.

During one of our many evening conversations, I asked Ahmer why he had chosen law. "Stanford Law School is very tough to get into," I said. "I heard that the acceptance rate is 9 percent. You must be brilliant."

"There are many people far more brilliant than me," he replied modestly. "Some of them are friends and acquaintances, and many of them applied but didn't get accepted. It's tough to get in if you are not focused. If you know what you want in life, no goal is far. I knew for a long time that I wanted to be a lawyer, because I believe in finding the truth and fighting for the truth. That's all."

He seemed somewhat pensive for a moment before he asked me, "So why do you want to be a journalist?"

I could not believe we were so alike. "If I tell you my reasons are exactly the same as yours, you won't believe me, but it's true. I want to seek the truth as well, mostly because that's what was so important to my father. His advice about speaking the truth has remained with me. It was the last pearl of wisdom he shared before he died; that's why I cherish it so much."

"I think that's splendid. It's a great profession, and I have a lot of respect for it."

Earlier that morning, Professor Reynolds had asked us to read a broad range of books. He had asked us to familiarize ourselves with literature from different eras and varied genres, and if possible, from other languages. "If you want to write, books are your fuel," he had said. "Remember you will always be a student, because no matter how well you write, there will always be a better version of what you have written. Write with a flow that is smooth so that even if you have written, rewritten, edited, and cut and pasted countless times, it appears as a consummation of a single thought, as if you never lifted your pen from the paper."

I asked Ahmer if he had any books in Urdu. The following day he brought me a whole collection of Urdu poetry, mostly the works of Faiz Ahmed Faiz. I thoroughly enjoyed reading them but needed help understanding many of the words. "I only studied Urdu until grade four," I said sheepishly, somewhat embarrassed at the paucity of my Urdu vocabulary.

"I can help you with some," he said with a smile.

Over the next few months, we spent considerable time dwelling over ageless poetry written by gifted poets. I knew I wanted to spend the rest of my life with Ahmer but was not sure how he felt about me. I hoped that my love would not be unrequited, as it often was in the heartfelt poetry we read. I was amazed at discovering what a hidden treasure Urdu poetry was.

"The youth of Pakistan is so engrossed in becoming westernized that they have forgotten to value their own assets," Ahmer said. When he tried to explain some of the more difficult poetry to me in English, he emphasized that the words lost their essence in translation. He was translating a well-known poem "Gar mujhe is ka yaqeen ho" and said, "I will try, though it's hard to bring out the meaning and I haven't studied Urdu at college level either."

"If you make a mistake, I won't catch it, so feel free," I said, eager to understand the poem.

His translation was beautiful:

If only I could have the belief
My companion, my friend
That the fatigue in your heart,
The sadness in your eyes,
The pain in your chest,
Can be erased by my care, my love,
That my words of comfort

Can be the remedy
That can bring life to your dull mind,
That can wash away the stains of insult from your fore-
head,
That can heal your diseased youth...
If only I could have the belief
Every day, morning, and night,
I would entertain you
I would sing songs to you
Light and sweet songs
Of waterfalls and springs
I would declare my love to you
I would go on singing, singing for your sake
I would go on weaving melodies
I would go on sitting before you for your sake
But my songs are not the remedy for your sadness,
For songs are not strong weapons, they are merely balms
for sorrow
And your sorrow cannot be healed without a weapon
A weapon that is not in my hands
Or the hands of any soul in this world
Except you.

Chapter 10

I went home that evening feeling overwhelmingly happy. It was true, then, that a song or a poem could change one's whole life. Ahmer was wrong if he believed he did not have the power to eradicate my sorrow, yet it was also true that the sadness in me was so profound that the weapon required to erase it completely was only within my reach.

Ahmer had changed me. He had given me a renewed zest for life, the gift of confidence, and countless memories that I would always cherish, even if, for some unforeseen reason things did not work out between us. My frightening dreams had dissipated to a significant degree. They had become rare and somewhat less intense. The nightmares had been replaced by happy dreams. I had a dream once of Ahmer and me riding a white horse along a snow-covered mountain path. He was riding fast, towards a new, bright sun, as if he were saving me from something and taking me to a happy place, a heaven on Earth. I felt it symbolized the way he had indeed saved me from a bitter existence, taken me away from all the darkness that had enveloped me for years towards a new sunrise.

When I attempted to return his poetry book, he said, "You've heard of the saying, haven't you, that the one who lends his book to someone is foolish, and the one who returns it is even more so?"

I had not heard it, so I smiled.

"I want to save you from foolishness, so please keep it."

It was the first gift I accepted from him.

He gave me a rose on my birthday, which I placed between the pages of the beautiful poem, along with the scrap of paper with Ahmer's handwritten translation. It was still wet from the water, so it left a red mark near the top of the page. Throughout my life, I often had a series of what-if questions running through my mind: What if my father hadn't been taken away from me? What if my mother had never remarried? But the positive person I was starting to rediscover in myself had begun asking questions in a different context. What if Professor Reynolds had not cancelled his class that day in February of the year before? If it had not been Papa's death anniversary, I probably would have gone back to my apartment to finish my laundry or get ahead of the schedule with my college assignments. Had Jennifer or Kavita been available, I may not have stayed alone on a bench reminiscing about the past. What if Ahmer had been having his class during that time? What if I had never struck up a conversation with him? What if I had never left Pakistan or he had never left? What if I had never met him? Introverted and conventional as I was, I probably would have never met anyone and simply agreed to marry whoever my mother and aunt chose for me. What if? But I believed that destiny would have brought us together regardless, if not in America then in Pakistan. We were meant to be, and nothing could ever come between us. I had been sure about a lot of things: leaving my home when I did, my career choice, Stanford. However, the conviction that Ahmer was right for me gave certainty a new meaning altogether.

I often thought that I might not have spoken to him had I met him in Pakistan. Here in America, his dark skin had drawn me to him; he had fulfilled my need to connect to someone from my country and my culture. Someone who understood me without the need to explain, without the need to translate my thoughts into words. I talked about Pakistan with my friends but I was always guarded, making every effort to highlight the positives and forever attempting to minimize—and sometimes disguise—the negatives. But with Ahmer it was different. It was like discussing the flaws of a beloved family member among family. I loved talking to him; it had become comfortable enough that it felt like walking home yet remained unpredictable enough that it felt like taking a different route every day.

One evening when it came time to walk back home, it suddenly started to rain. What began as a light drizzle soon transitioned into a heavy downpour. I stood under the arches to wait for it to slow down, but it did not. The oak trees that had previously given me refuge appeared helpless in this stormy, thunderous rain. Ahmer had an umbrella and said he would be more than happy to walk me home. We waited for a little while longer, and when it subsided a bit, I gladly accepted his offer. He insisted I take the umbrella, so part of the way we shared it, and when the rain became less intense, he held it generously over my head, ensuring that neither my books, nor my hair got wet. Thereafter, even on the brightest, sunniest days, he walked me home.

We had many light conversations and on occasion would have long heart-to-heart talks. We would stroll beneath the shade of the tall palm trees and gaze at the bright pink magnolias that crossed our path. I had walked that path countless times before having met Ahmer, but everything seemed much more beautiful and serene in his presence. I appreciated the lush green of the grass beneath my feet and the sunshine peeking through the trees over my head. I noticed the birds chirping and the squirrels stealthily climbing up the branches before mysteriously disappearing from view. The walk home had once seemed tedious; walking alone, thoughts of my past would come back to haunt me, and by the time I reached home, my feet would be tired and my mind would be worn out. Now that same walk seemed too short and made me wish that I lived further away. Our walks had become a perfect way to wrap up my day. I returned home feeling positive and worthwhile. Our friendship made perfect sense, much like the numbers and letters in a solved algebra equation, the time we spent together concluding like a well-constructed sentence.

On one of our walks, I finally gathered the courage to broach the subject that had been dominating my thoughts for months. "So are you taken?"

"Taken where? Taken aback, taken to prison, or taken for granted?" He was always being funny and it was impossible to outwit him.

"You know what I mean, Ahmer."

"No, but I am considering you very strongly."

I could not help but laugh, and although I was not sure if he was joking, I let it be. I liked the way this was playing out. I just knew I felt happy and complete. He was a true gentleman who had a lot of respect for women, a generous heart, and the best advice.

On a day when I was feeling particularly down, he said to me, "It is natural to feel sadness about your father. He was taken away from you at such a tender age, but maybe you can try to do what I do when I think of my mother: think of all the good years and the wonderful memories. Don't let the tragedy of his untimely death overshadow his whole life. You are such a wonderful person; I'm sure much of the credit goes to him, and the thing he would have wanted most is for you to be happy. You are a giving person, Sana, and one cannot give from a heart full of sadness and anger."

I thought about Ahmer's advice very carefully. What he had said was so deep and so true; his words worked wonders for me, becoming a soothing balm on my aching heart. I am sure they made me a better person, or at least they brought out the good person that had, years ago, died somewhere inside me.

Chapter 11

Two thousand and one was the year of my graduation. I had been accepted for the journalism program at Stanford, and Ahmer had joined the master's program for law. Ahmer had become a vital part of my existence. We had become inseparable friends who could read one another like pages of a thoroughly memorized book, and hear one another as lyrics of a song practiced to perfection. Neither of us had given a name to our friendship, and it was adequate for me that he was my companion and my confidante.

My aunt and uncle were present for my graduation ceremony, as were Ammi and Sahir. Sara had wanted to attend, but my stepfather did not let her. I was disappointed that my sister was not part of such an important day in my life, and it added another level of resentment to what I already felt for Mr. Rehman.

I embraced my education and immersed myself in the world of journalism. Ahmer had unlocked so much inside me that I was able to overcome countless obstacles and find new avenues of writing. I stopped worrying about what people would think or how they would judge me based on what I wrote. I felt free and was ready to venture into new territory like a caterpillar having acquired its butterfly wings.

I was fortunate to have great teachers who taught me lessons that extended beyond the words that were written in my textbooks. Professor Reynolds once said,

"Always pay attention to detail. If you write facts, make sure it is the truth—not just the apparent truth, but the real truth. Be inquisitive. Check all your facts. Always read between the lines and hear what's between the audible frequencies. Don't go by what's on the surface; dig deeper. Dig until you find the truth, because even if it isn't what you expected to find, it is your real treasure. If you write fiction, write it as a truth so it appears real; that means you don't just write it, you live it. You sleep thinking about it. You dream about it. If you are writing about a person, you have to become that person. If you are writing about a place, your mind has to be in that place. You want to be like a seasoned actor performing a character role. Write what your heart tells you to and when it tells you to, and I promise the ink will flow."

Ahmer was getting busier with his college work, as well, but always managed to find time for me. "You seem to be praying a lot these days," he said to me on one occasion. "Can you add me to your prayer list?"

"I don't have to add you," I said, smiling. "You're already on it." You are on the top of the list, I thought to myself. "Anything special I should ask for?"

"I desperately want to get chosen for that law firm internship in New York I told you about. It's very competitive; they select only four law students from the entire country."

"I will remember to include that request in my prayers, but I'm sure your outstanding credentials will get you there, *Inshallah* [God willing]."

A few weeks later, Ahmer called and said, "I got selected for the internship in New York! I can't believe it. I'm so excited and had to call you right away."

"That's great news," I said, feeling genuinely proud of his achievement. "Congratulations. I know what a promising lawyer you are because I can never win an argument with you. You have such immense convincing power that the jury will always be on your side." However, as I spoke, the thought of Ahmer leaving for the East Coast began to tug at me.

"Thank you for praying, Sana," he said softly.

"I can't say I prayed day and night, but I did pray with a good amount of sincerity, even though it means you are going to be far. That was the least I could do after you took away my stage fright so successfully. How long is the internship?" I asked, not wanting to sound overly devastated about our forthcoming separation.

"It's six weeks long and it starts two weeks from now."

"New York has a culture of its own, you know. People talk fast, and you might not be able to understand them. They walk fast, too—they could run you over," I said, attempting to neutralize my sadness with some humor.

"I'm not worried about getting run over. I always walk looking down, so I am always grounded. People who keep their chin too high are the ones who fall," he replied cleverly.

"But if you look down, you might not see all the beauty. You don't want to miss the magnificence of the Twin Towers or the pretty women on the streets."

"I will make sure I see the Twin Towers; actually, I'll be working there. Pretty women I don't need to see. After all, it's not like I'm searching anymore." He had won his argument elegantly once again, and since I was flattered by what he had said, I gladly decided to rest my case.

The two weeks leading up to his departure passed before I knew it. When he was about to leave for the airport, I wished him good luck. "Take care of yourself," was the last thing he said to me before he left. In that moment I suddenly felt that he would be gone for a really long time. It's just six weeks, I reminded myself.

His schedule in New York was busier than I had imagined, and I felt as if his life had taken up the city's pace. He seemed to be working extra hard and eating and sleeping progressively less.

"I am enjoying my work a lot," he told me over the phone. "They like me and they might offer me a position in the future if I do well. But Sana, I'm so bored without you. I tell you about my day and all over the phone, but it's just not the same. I can't believe I had gotten so used to your company. I've known you for five years, but it feels like an eternity. I can't remember what life was like without you."

Neither could I. The sun seemed to dim and the moon became gray in his absence. Songs sounded less melodious and the sketches in Jennifer's gallery seemed to lose their luster. The walks from home to college and back seemed endless, and the few remaining magnolias lining the path seemed less fragrant, as if Ahmer had taken their scent with him. I tried to bury myself in writing articles for the paper and for the college newsletter but could only seem to come up with unsatisfactory drafts that appeared amateurish and inarticulately written. Some days I would write for hours, reconstructing sentences and rearranging paragraphs, but was never satisfied with the finished product. On other days I would simply stare at the linear shadows on the carpet, cast by the blinds, struggling to overcome my writer's block. The redwood trees outside my window appeared haggard, their dark brown barks wrinkled and peeling as if they had suddenly started to show their age. Life seemed to have lost its joy and its spirit.

I was counting the days until his return and had started marking my calendar. I missed him tremendously. I told him I would pick him up at the airport, but later he decided it would be too early in the morning. Besides, I had a class that morning and was scheduled to give an important presentation. He was flying to San Francisco, and would take the BART from there to Palo Alto.

"After my class, we have to go celebrate your return and your big achievement working with such an honorable firm. I am proud of you," I said.

"I am all yours as soon as I land in California," he replied.

Distance had served to bring us closer, and I was beginning to realize the magnitude of the effect Ahmer had on my being. His words greatly influenced my thoughts. He made me realize that I was indeed a good person inside—a person who my father would have been proud of—but that I needed to remove the bitter layer that defined my exterior. I loved him and had also started to love and rediscover myself. I had seen friends with broken hearts from ruined relationships and had always tried to protect myself from such betrayal and hurt. Ahmer understood that about me and was very respectful of the emotional distance I wished to maintain, treading slowly and cautiously. He knew that he was the source of my happiness but that there was a sad part of me that he might never reach.

"If only I knew how to wipe away your last tear, I would," he would say. "But I can't. It made me feel helpless before, but now I have learned to accept that tear as part of you. I just want you to know that I will always be there for you, and your happiness means the world to me."

He's coming tomorrow, I thought with a smile. I had made plans for a sumptuous lunch at his favorite restaurant, followed by dessert, ice cream perhaps. I thought I might finally be able to order blueberry ice cream, a flavor I had abandoned since February 11, 1987. I thought it might actually taste sweet again.

I went to bed early, but a nightmare woke me up. It had come back again after quite a long interval and was more disturbing than ever. Ahmer was in it. He was running toward me and was covered in blood. I was screaming and then suddenly woke up. My shirt was drenched with sweat. It was three in the morning, and I was horrified by Ahmer's appearance in my nightmare; it was so frightening and unnerving. I went back to sleep, my alarm set for seven-thirty, but I was awoken abruptly by the ringing of the phone before my alarm went off. I glanced over at the clock and saw that it was seven o'clock. Ahmer must have boarded the plane by now, I thought. Maybe his flight was delayed or something. Maybe my mother was calling from Pakistan and had not realized it was so early here. Perhaps Sahir had a problem he wished to discuss with me right away. It was an unrecognizable number. I picked it up, and it was Jennifer, who had been visiting her father in Michigan for the fall. The instant I heard her voice, I knew something was wrong.

"Were you up yet?" she said, her voice was quivering.

"I was about to wake up. What's wrong? Are you OK?"

"A lot has happened in America this morning, Sana. Please stay calm and turn the news on. Two passenger planes have crashed into the Twin Towers. They are saying it might be a terrorist attack. I wasn't sure what Ahmer's plans were so I called you. Don't be alarmed. I'm sure he'll be all right."

I could not believe what I was hearing. This could not be happening. Ahmer was not supposed to be at work that day, but his flight had left that morning. I was assimilating all the information that Jennifer had given me and simultaneously tuning into CNN.

I did not know what to do at first. I was panicking, and I could feel my heart racing faster than ever. I jumped out of bed and called Ahmer's cell phone, but there was no answer. I called several times in quick succession. Then I realized he must be on his flight and could not possibly be available to answer his phone. The video of the planes crashing into the towers was being replayed again and again, and each time it seemed so unreal. If Ahmer had been in his office that day, he might be among those hundreds of people who had lost their lives to these senseless attacks.

News continued to pour in about a third plane that had crashed into the Pentagon, and within minutes there was news about a fourth plane that had crashed into a hillside in Pennsylvania. I felt reassured that Ahmer could not have been on any of those flights but then wondered if it was selfish of me to want nothing more at that moment than for Ahmer to be alive and safe. What about all those people and their family members who were trying to come to terms with this awful tragedy? My heart was crying for each and every one of them. But if anything were to happen to Ahmer, my heart would surely stop beating. I could not possibly go on with my life. I went over to the kitchen to get a glass of water from the refrigerator, and Jennifer's sketch of the towers caught my eye. I looked away and went back to watching the television.

Within minutes, more details started pouring in. The plane that had crashed in Pennsylvania was United Flight 93, which had left from New York and was headed to San Francisco. Headed to San Francisco. This morning. The glass of water dropped from my hand, and tiny pieces of glass scattered all over the floor. Faster than lightening, I went to pull out the piece of paper from my drawer where I had casually scribbled Ahmer's flight details. I remembered the airline, but not the number. Please God, please don't let it be 93. Anything but 93, I silently pleaded. Ahmer, you have to live a long life. You have to live for me.

My head was pounding, and my hands were trembling. My forehead was covered in a cold sweat. I thought of the dream I had had a few hours before and Ahmer's role in it; he had been covered in blood. I felt a knot in my stomach and a heavy weight on my chest, as if a sandbag had been tied around me. My throat was burning, and I wanted to scream, but my voice was gone. The memory of the worst moment of my life returned, like a vivid flashback, and I wished that I was not alone. For what seemed like the longest three minutes of my life, I could not find the paper. I quickly threw out all the items from my drawer, but it was not there. I soon remembered that I had taken it out of the drawer and placed it in my purse a few days before. It had to be the black purse, as I had not used the beige one in a week at least. I wished I had inherited some organizational skills from my mother.

Oh, why did it have so many compartments? A front pocket and a side pocket? And why had I not cleared it of all the unnecessary paraphernalia? I emptied the contents all over the bed. As I sifted through them, I felt the knot in my stomach grow tighter. Among the items on the bed were my car keys, my lipstick, my sunglasses, a receipt from Safeway, a Stanford student coupon for the Jing-Jing Chinese restaurant that Ahmer and I frequented, an unused tissue, a black ball-point pen, notes from the first draft of an article I had just written, my wallet, and a pack of chewing gum. I did not care about any of these things right now. Finally I found what I had been looking for. I said a prayer, opened up the crumpled paper, and there it was, written in dark black ink that had smudged a little, partly encircled by a stain from the bottom of a cup of tea: *United Flight 93.*

I let out a loud scream. Ahmer was dead. This had to be a nightmare, part of the horrible dream I had been having some hours ago. Please, someone wake me up. Wake me up to a reality that is beautiful and a life that includes a future with Ahmer. I looked up at the clock and fumbled for the phone as the blaring television continued to relay the morning's tragic events. I called United Airlines to check the passenger list but was put on hold, so I placed it on speaker.

Was this how short-lived my happiness was going to be? If, by some miracle, he had not boarded that plane, he would have called me to tell me he was alive. So it was over. My father had lost his precious life to greed, and Ahmer had lost his to violence and insanity. Why had I come into this world? To love and to lose? Was that the purpose of my life? I could not live anymore. What had I done that had been so wrong, so deserving of such a cruel punishment? First God had taken my father away. It had taken me fourteen years to be able to say his name without shedding a tear. I had not recovered yet from the first tragedy of my life and was finally getting to a point where I had allowed myself to be happy again. It had taken me years, and now I was dead all over again. Ahmer had been my lifeline, my golden ray of hope in the blackest dark.

Ahmer was in the prime of his life with a bright future before him. How could this be? He had never been to New York before and was there because of his outstanding academic achievements; his brilliance had put him there, on that plane. My prayers had put him there. If only I had not spent so many days praying for this selection, if I had just prayed for whatever was best. Why did I always wish for the wrong things? But inside a voice was telling me that my faith dictated to accept that God had decided when we would leave this Earth. Ahmer's time had been three minutes past ten o'clock, Eastern Standard Time, in the morning on September 11, 2001. I had to accept it. I would never see him again or hear his voice again. If only I could hear his voice one more time. If only I could have said to him what I had felt for him.

"Take care of yourself" had been his parting words to me, as if he knew it was a final good-bye. But I don't want to take care of myself; I don't know how to anymore. I want you to take care of me, Ahmer. I picked up my cell phone and listened to his saved voice message from two days before.

"I looked through the windows of one of the towers and saw many pretty faces. But the prettiest one is thousands of miles away."

News kept pouring in about who was behind this. The phrases "intelligence failure," "security breach," "Muslim extremists," and "Osama bin Laden" were repeated by newscasters and terrorism experts from around the world. This was not religion. This was not Islam. This was insanity.

"All forty-four passengers aboard Flight 93 are presumed dead."

"Remains of the victims…" they said. *Remains.* So that's what it was going to be. There would not even be a body to bury.

Jennifer kept calling me and leaving frantic messages, but I did not have the courage to talk to anyone. I sat motionless on the couch for an unknown duration. I stared blankly outside the window of my apartment. Everything seemed still, as if there was fear in the air. A dewdrop sat hesitantly at the edge of a leaf like a newly formed tear too scared to fall. I had the urge to shut off the television, as if not hearing the news would somehow save me from the reality I was struggling to deny. I turned it off for a few seconds, but the silence was unbearable and the thirst to know unquenchable, so I switched it back on.

I thought of calling Phuppo or Ammi, but how could they feel my pain when they did not even know who Ahmer was? The moon would never shine bright on me again. I would never feel the warmth of the sun or smell the fragrance of the flowers again. All the melody in my life would disappear. The symphony that I had compared my life to would be reduced to the lowest octave and become unharmonious, unchanging, and mundane. I was in a state of shock and for a moment contemplated jumping out the window. But not only was suicide selfish and cowardly, it was also sinful. The ringing of the doorbell suddenly interrupted my thoughts. I ran toward the door and stepped on a piece of broken glass on the carpet but did not feel the pain of the bleeding cut on the sole of my foot because when I opened the door, a miracle greeted me. It was Ahmer standing in the doorway.

Chapter 12

God had been kind to me. God only gives us as much grief as we can bear, it is said, and in that moment I believed it with all my heart. I would not have been able to recover from a second loss so utterly devastating.

Ahmer had taken an earlier flight. He had actually flown in the night before so he could see me sooner. He too had been asleep in the morning and had not heard the news or the ring of his cell phone. When he finally woke up, he learned what had happened and immediately walked over. He tried to call but was unable to get through because both my phones had been on hold with United Airlines. No words can describe the degree of relief and gratitude I felt. Ahmer had changed plans, or perhaps God had changed his plans for him.

The attacks shook us up and made us realize how precious and fragile a human life really is. Among the remains, victims' lipsticks had been found; lipsticks that had outlived their wearers, as had the paper and plastic of passports that helped confirm the identities of the deceased. It was an overwhelmingly sad day, and my heart bled for all of those who had died and their families. I was angered by this radical distortion of my religion by the terrorists. Over the next week, it was said that 2,970 people had died, including hundreds of firefighters. I cried for days after seeing pictures of the deceased and hearing their stories. Ahmer was shocked to learn that many people he had worked with in the Twin Towers were among the dead. I was deeply saddened because not only was it a tragedy for America, it was a tragedy for the world.

A week later, Ahmer and I were walking our usual path and discussing all that had come to light about the 9/11 catastrophe. Nearly three thousand had perished, and the victims had been from all over the world—ninety countries to be exact. The nineteen hijackers had been identified, and Osama bin Laden had become the most wanted individual on FBI's list. My thoughts suddenly went to that day and I looked at Ahmer and thought: It was probably for thirty minutes, Ahmer, that I thought I had lost you for good, but it seemed like days. I had not felt this kind of anguish in a long, long time. It made me realize how precious your existence is to me. I really could not have lived my life without you.

"What were you thinking?" he asked

"Just how lucky I am, how truly blessed, and how fragile and precious life is."

We talked in depth for a while about all the events. On September 20, President George W. Bush declared a "war on terror" and announced a plan to invade Afghanistan. He said, "Our response involves far more than instant retaliation and isolated strikes. Americans should not expect one battle but a lengthy campaign unlike any other we have ever seen."

By mid-October I had decided what my thesis was going to be about. The 9/11 tragedy had changed the world around us, and I wanted to find clarity for myself in these confusing times. In a meeting with President Bush, Pervaiz Musharraf, who had been leading Pakistan for the last two years after overthrowing the Nawaz Shareef regime in yet another bloodless coup, alleged his unflinching support to counter terrorism, thus forming a unique political alliance between the United States and Pakistan.

The barely visible colors of Palo Alto's hesitant fall had arrived, and our conversations were intermingled with the crunching of the perished leaves beneath our feet as we walked toward my home.

"I need your input for my thesis article," I said to Ahmer. I had already told him about the title, which was, "How 9/11 Changed America and How it Changed Me: A Muslim's Perspective." I felt that the moderate Muslims were losing their voice in all the noise, and it needed to be heard. I certainly did not agree with the terrorists or understand their motivation, but I did not agree with unchecked military aggression either. I did not believe that violence was justified in any form, by anyone. I was on humanity's side—a side that unfortunately almost always lost.

"Sure, I'll give you my input. You're the writer, though."

"I try to be the writer, but you are the thinker. The problem with being a writer is that one tends to be more imaginative than objective, and this is about emotion for me, especially because my emotions were directly involved on 9/11, but it needs to be factual."

A voice inside me reminded me of my father. I had never told Ahmer that he had been killed or that I had witnessed his murder. I told him he had died in a car accident. I had forced myself not to think about it but had not been entirely successful. I thought that discussing it with Ahmer might make my wounds bleed again. And since I had only recently been able to laugh again, I was not eager to unearth my buried memories just yet.

However, I was planning to spend the rest of my life with this wonderful person, and I knew that if I did not share this last detail, it would be like hiding a whole part of who I was. It was the last tear that Ahmer had insightfully recognized in my eye. It had taken a lot of work on his end to crack the shell of my hard exterior and scrape away the bitterness from within me. He had managed to take away a good amount of it, but if I failed to share with him the whole truth, he would not be able to get any further.

Ahmer and I finally went for our ice cream outing on New Year's Eve. I had only a scoop of blueberry on a cone, having joined the club of the weight conscious over the last few years.

I would jog on the treadmill in the college gym a few times a week, although I found it to be painfully boring unless Jennifer accompanied me. Part of the cone fell, creating an unsightly stain on my sleeve. In the past, dropping ice cream on my new sweater would have caused me to mourn the lost ice cream more than the stained sweater. However, now that my appearance had started to matter to me, I did not regret the calories that had been deducted from my dessert. The ice cream tasted sweet despite the fact that it froze my jaw with the cold wind hitting my face, and despite the memories it unleashed of the worst day of my life.

Ahmer walked me home, and as I turned around to leave, he handed me a small box in striped silver wrapping paper tied with a curly silver ribbon. By the unevenness of it, I knew he had wrapped it himself, and I was touched by his effort.

"Open it when you get home," he said.

This had been the tradition we had followed with gifts, although we had only exchanged a few. I was in a hurry to unwrap the present but did not fail to notice that the sky had filled up with the twinkle of countless stars. The box was small enough that it could hold a ring, but it was not square. I reminded myself not to harbor any unrealistic expectations. We were friends—exceptionally good friends. I rushed inside and opened the box. It was an iPod. A small card attached to it read, "So that every song is at your fingertips, so that there is more melody in your life."

I called Ahmer and told him that it was the best present I had ever received. After washing the ice cream stain from my sweater, I began organizing all my songs and basking in the glory of my new music addiction. I started going gladly to the gym, even on days that Jennifer was not available, because I could listen to all the songs I wanted and run to their beat. Apple and Steve Jobs were in the heart of Silicon Valley, creating history right next door.

I often looked at the card Ahmer had given me and thought to myself, *there is more melody in my life, but it's not because of the iPod.*

Over the next several months, Ahmer bought me other presents, each one thoughtfully wrapped in the same striped silver wrapping paper, successively acquiring the touch of a practiced hand. One of his small cards attached to the present said, "Life is a truth waiting to be unfolded, a gift waiting to be unwrapped."

One weekend afternoon in the winter of 2002, on our way back from having watched and enjoyed the first showing of *A Beautiful Mind*, our conversation turned to my family.

"Sana, you should make peace with your mother. I know you have gone through a lot, and losing your father at such a young age is a tragedy no one should have to face. But I am telling you as your friend and as a person who has lost both parents, don't be angry with your mother. You are so lucky she is alive and healthy. Mama suffered a lot. I tried to do everything for her, and she was a fighter, but at the end, there was nothing anyone could do. Her disease was stable on different kinds of treatments for three years, but then it spread everywhere, including her brain. In the last week of her life, she didn't even recognize me. She was on a morphine drip at home through a pump to control the pain in her bones. I prayed for her suffering to end."

He knew about the resentment I felt toward my mother for remarrying and my sadness over my lost closeness with my brother. He continued to give me a new perspective and made me realize how different things appeared from every angle. He said, "If there are two people looking out the window of a car, they will always see things differently, especially if one is a child and the other is an adult. The child may see the flying birds and the setting sun, but the adult will see the car that is too close. Children think in a much more simplistic fashion and cannot always comprehend adult emotions."

"But sometimes adults need to think like a child to understand what trauma a child is going through, because his or her feelings need validation, Ahmer."

"You are right, Sana. Maybe your mother should have asked you before remarrying or given you enough time to accept everything."

That was something I admired about him so much; even when he did not agree with me, he always gave credence to my feelings.

"But I don't think it's fair to put all the blame on her. She was almost as young as you are now. Can you imagine what it was like for her to have lost a husband, a provider, the father of her children at that age? She did not have a college degree, had never worked, had never signed a check, and had not known life without a man's protection."

"But she didn't even ask for me to return. When she had Sara, she didn't need me anymore because she had found a prettier, more loyal replacement of me," I said. Ahmer looked at me and smiled. "Come on, Sana, I can't believe the thoughts that you let thrive in your otherwise mature mind. Mothers love all their children just the same; you know that. Every child has a special place in their mother's heart."

"It's easy for you to say that; you are an only child." I realized I was being argumentative and unreasonable, but he knew that his words were slowly repairing the damage inside me.

"OK, I have something a little harsh to say. I will only say it if you want to hear it. Otherwise we can talk about something else, like what was on yesterday's Oprah, or which movies deserve the Oscar this year, or whether the political situation in Pakistan is ever going to get better, or this news about war on Iraq."

"I do have to give my Oscar opinion now that you brought it up. I think Russell Crowe was outstanding today; he could win

an Oscar for that role, but then so could Sean Penn for *I Am Sam.*
OK, go on."

"I liked both movies tremendously, but I liked *Beautiful Mind* better because I watched it with you," he said.

"As for the war on Iraq, the president states that his intelligence has notified him about weapons of mass destruction. But any war to me is sad. It seldom solves any problems and simply serves to create more poverty, famine, loss of innocent life, and resentment at multiple levels."

"So you are putting off the discussion about your family?" Ahmer persisted.

"No, I'm sorry. I know whatever you say will make sense to me—not necessarily at that moment, but sometimes days or months later. Go ahead, I'm listening."

"You know what I think? I think your anger is a little bit mixed in with some remorse that you bear for leaving your mother and brother behind. Don't you think it was hard for your mother to have her daughter oceans away and have to worry constantly about her well-being? Don't you think your brother missed you or failed to understand why you just left without explaining anything to him?"

Who was he to judge me, I thought; he did not know my circumstances or my family. But then his words struck a chord. As usual, his analysis had been accurate. I wondered why he was a lawyer and not a psychologist.

"I feel that my mother is alive within me and I talk to her, tell her about my day. It helps me lead a more fulfilling life. The heartache is always there but it becomes so much easier to bear, Sana. I always try to live my life without regrets. I do have one regret though."

"What?" I said, wondering how such a content person could have any regrets.

"That I didn't meet you sooner." He looked at me with fondness in his eyes.

I felt too shy to say anything aloud but I knew that Ahmer still heard me. I went home and treated myself to a microwavable Lean Cuisine dinner. I sat on the couch, flipping through television channels, unable to find anything that deserved my undivided attention. With Ahmer's words echoing in my mind, I decided to call my mother that night.

When we spoke, she told me that Zareen was pregnant with her second child and that Sahir had given up a chance to play a regional cricket match because it would compromise his studies. Sara was giving her a hard time as a stubborn teenager. Well, at least she had waited until her teenage years before causing trouble, I thought to myself. Suddenly she remarked that someone had expressed an interest in sending me a marriage proposal.

"His name is Zain," she said. He had completed his MBA and was currently employed by a prestigious bank in Karachi. He wished to get settled, and the family was helping him search for a suitable bride. Not only was there an endless thread of concerned relatives serving as co-conspirators, but Zain's mother had turned out to be Ammi's old classmate as well. He was ambitious and enterprising and wished to further his education in America and fine-tune his career to meet the challenges of the new world. He was looking for someone who could understand and support his aspirations.

"It is a perfect match," our families had unilaterally decided. I was upset and did not say much to my mother over the phone, but I mentioned it to Ahmer the following morning, and he told me not to worry. That was all he said, but in his eyes that day, I saw an unspoken promise.

Chapter 13

The summer of 2002 arrived, and I continued to wait earnestly for Ahmer's unspoken promise to turn into a marriage proposal. After my final exams, we went to see the Indian Movie *Devdas*, which was a remake of an older version. It was a beautiful movie with fantastic music. There was a scene where the girl, played by the stunning Aishwariya Rai, got married to someone she did not love, under pressure from her family. The man she loved, Devdas, played by the famous Shahrukh Khan, bade her a sad farewell. He lived next door, so he participated in the wedding, helping to carry the palanquin in which she departed, while a tragic song played in the background. It was such a touching scene that my eyes filled with tears. I let a few escape silently, hoping Ahmer would not notice.

On the way home, we discussed the film, and I said, "It was so tragic, her getting married that way. It must be so hard to marry someone when you love another. I felt bad for both of them."

"Yeah, but it was all his fault. He didn't propose to her in time, so he lost her, ruining her life and his own. He didn't fight for her. And then he was so self-destructive; he became a drunkard, destroyed his liver, and died," he said, as if he were talking about a real person.

"I thought it was a beautiful ending," I said, "especially the scene where he was dying at the doorstep of her enormous mansion, and she ran to see who it was, but the gates closed on her before she could meet him."

"So you like tragic endings, then," Ahmer said with a smile.

"Sometimes. They touch your heart. But only in stories, not in real life."

After saying good-bye to Ahmer, I walked up to my apartment, wondering what the conclusion of our story was going to be. I gazed up at the sky, said a prayer in my heart, and admired the full moon shining down on me in all its glory.

Upon completing my journalism degree in 2002, I accepted a position at the local news station where I had interned and continued to write articles for the paper. I also volunteered periodically to give lectures to undergraduate students at Stanford. Ahmer still had several months to go before completing his combined law and business master's degree, and that helped me finalize my decision to stay in Palo Alto.

I soon began working on a documentary for television based on my thesis article on 9/11. I had conducted some interviews to write the thesis, and I used them as a starting point to develop my project further. I intended to record some interviews in Pakistan as well, to capture the diverse opinions among various factions and to address the escalated violence since 9/11. In the meantime, I continued my job with anchoring and occasional spot reporting.

In 2003, news channels and papers were inundated with rumors of CIA leaks and allegations against George Bush regarding the dearth of evidence to support the presence of weapons of mass destruction, which had been the pretext of the invasion of Iraq.

I had not visited Pakistan the year before, mainly because I had been terrified of having to meet Zain. Sahir was in medical school and was immersed in his studies. I did not think I would be graced by much of his company if I went home. He rarely had time to even talk to me over the phone. Occasionally he would call and mumble something for a few minutes, his mind constantly filled with the cardiovascular physiology he had read about or the countless names of bones and muscles he had memorized the night before. He was not getting enough sleep, and per Ammi and Sara's accounts, had lost a considerable amount of weight. I was proud of him, as I was sure my father would have been had he lived to see this day, but worried at the same time. I e-mailed him words that I had read on one of my college clipboards: "Kill the stress before the stress kills you, reach the goal before the goal kicks you, help others before someone helps you, live life before life leaves you."

Sara spent most of her holidays with her paternal aunt in Lahore, so I did not see the benefit of going every summer. It would be impossible to avoid conversations with my stepfather, as Ammi would be the only buffer and possibly not a very effective one.

I had known and cared for Ahmer for several years by then, and it worried me sometimes that he had not broached the subject of marriage. I tried not to think about it too much and just let the tune play itself out. I was afraid that asking him about it prematurely might compromise our friendship, which was too precious for me to risk; it would be like gambling with the last coin I had left.

One spring evening, we were sitting in the quad laughing over a recent *Everybody Loves Raymond* episode. We were snacking on salt and vinegar Pringles, which I had allowed myself to occasionally indulge in, while sipping on our cans of Diet Coke. "It was hilarious how Robert purposely spoiled all the wedding preparations so Amy wouldn't ask him to do any more work," I said.

"Yeah, and Raymond and his dad were the ones who put him up to it."

We continued to share unimportant, yet interesting details of our every day life. I noticed that Ahmer seemed preoccupied and that faraway look in his eyes had returned. As I saw the hint of the purple jacarandas emerging from the tips of the tall trees, my mind drifted back to all the springs we had shared together. As I sat there trying to decipher his thoughts, his voice suddenly transitioned to a serious tone. "The other day I was talking to Mama's picture," he said, pausing for a few seconds. "I was talking to my mom's picture," he repeated, clearing his throat as though he were struggling to formulate the words he wanted to say, "as I often do, and I told her that some years ago, I had met a wonderful girl."

"Really?" I asked, my eyes wide with amazement, my tone that of one requesting confirmation. "What else did you tell her?"

"That she makes me smile, that I have fallen for her, and that I am going to ask her what I have intended to ask her since the day we first met. I will ask her to marry me."

Considering how compatible we were, how much we cared for each other, and how we both knew that marriage would be the next step, I had expected a proposal for a long time. But I had not expected it at that moment, not when we were sitting in the quad munching on Pringles and sipping Diet Coke. The place was definitely right—it was where we had first met. I looked at the ground that had a puddle of water, a slowly disappearing remnant of the morning rainfall. In it, I could see my reflection and Ahmer's. We looked good together, as if we were meant to be. I had become increasingly apprehensive about getting tied into a matrimonial knot with a stranger and having to say yes in lieu of not having sufficient grounds to do otherwise. If I had a proposal from a well-educated person from a respectable family, my mother would not force me into marrying someone I did not know at all.

It was one of the happiest moments of my life. I had been so hurt by all that had happened in my past that the fear of betrayal had stopped me from becoming close to anyone. It had happened nevertheless, and I had rediscovered the power of human closeness and the timelessness of unconditional love. In that instant, I felt the disillusionment I had harbored in my mind for years drifting away and the sadness I had sheltered in my heart melting away. I was daring to be happy again.

"Will you marry me, Sana?" I looked up into his eyes, but before I could say yes, he stopped me.

"Before you answer, I want to tell you something about myself, something that I have not yet shared with you. I don't think we should have any secrets now. For you to understand me fully, I want to take you to meet someone. And for that we need to go to Pakistan. If things work out, we can have an engagement or a wedding right there."

He took a beautiful ring from his pocket. It was a traditional ring made of pure gold, with emeralds and rubies forming a flower in the center. "It's my mother's," he said.

"She asked me to give it to the girl I marry. Keep it with you, but don't wear it until you make your final decision."

"It's beautiful, Ahmer," I said, tears of happiness filling my eyes. I looked at the ring with admiration. I felt honored that I was the chosen one, the one who, in his eyes, deserved to be the wearer of his beloved mother's ring. I was also surprised and did not know how to interpret all of Ahmer's words. I tried not to overanalyze them, but my joy was dampened by the revelation that Ahmer had hidden something from me. Was it fair of me to hold that against him when I had done the same? My secret was dark, but not something that could change anything between us. But what if Ahmer's secret, once revealed, came directly in the way of our happiness? How would I bear it? Had he not once told me that life was a gift waiting to be unwrapped? And I had begun to tear away the wrappings of hurt and anger and rediscover the beauty of this finite journey called life. But what secret was hidden inside this person I thought I knew so well? What if, after removing the shiny silver wrapping, an unbecoming truth emerged?

I told Kavita about it, and she tried to allay my fears. She was always the trusting one and held Ahmer in the highest esteem.

"You are a psychologist, Kavita," I said to her. "Tell me what you make of this. Do you think I should worry?"

"No, you should not," she replied with a reassuring smile on her face. "You have known him for years; we have all known him for years. He's a good person and he cares about you a lot. If there is something he wants to tell you, just let him say it rather than worrying needlessly."

Jennifer was a little more circumspect, and I could see it in her eyes. She decided against saying much. She congratulated me for the proposal but did not meet my gaze when I asked for her interpretation of Ahmer's words. The more I thought about it, the more it troubled me. Perhaps he had a past. If he had loved someone before me, I could not hold that against him. After all he had not been committed to me then. What if he had been married before? What if he was still married? It was not against the law in Pakistan to have more than one wife. The day we had met and reminisced about Pakistan, he had given an interesting analogy about his relationship with Pakistan being like a marriage. I had been surprised that an unmarried person could talk in depth about the various stages of marriage.

The more I thought about it, the more I felt my heart slamming like a hammer against my chest wall. What if he had a child or children? It could be his child he wanted me to meet. That would certainly be a hindrance to our wedding. Even if I could overlook a marriage, could I overlook the fact that he had hidden such a significant truth from me? I had not accepted my stepfather in so many years. Could I possibly accept a stepson or daughter? They would have preconceived dislike for me if I were going to replace their mother. They surely would resent me. Would I be able to raise them as my own? I paused and then answered my own question: I could. I would.

My mind went back to the turmoil of emotions I had felt on 9/11. Anything would be acceptable to me except being permanently separated from Ahmer. But how would I convince my mother and my aunt that this was the person I had chosen for myself? How would I convince them that he was indeed the one for me, the one who would justify my refusal of Zain's proposal?

My mother would have difficulty accepting that I had chosen a husband for myself. I was only beginning to realize that I might have been unfair to her and that I may have disappointed her as a child. Would it be fair to fail her as an adult as well? Was that the daughter I wanted to be? The daughter that my father had said was destined to do great things, destined to make him proud. I paused for a moment and realized that everything that had wreaked havoc in my mind for the past hour was mere speculation. I was a journalist—a fact-finder, a truth-seeker—and here I was, solving a puzzle without having the pieces, capturing a photograph with a faulty lens. I had to trust Ahmer. Despite the nagging sense of doubt, I felt that his intentions were good; that was why he had asked me not to give him an answer to his marriage proposal. Had he not given me that opportunity, I would have answered in the affirmative without the blink of an eye, without the bat of an eyelash.

I had already planned to be in Pakistan for my vacation, and Ahmer was to arrive a week later. My stepfather, being in real estate, had found a good bargain, and the family was moving into a new home. I had asked them to wait for my arrival so I could help out with the relocation, and they had gladly complied.

Two years had elapsed since 9/11, but my fear of flying had not dissipated. I read *The Kite Runner* on the plane, which was Ahmer's most recent gift. He had scribbled "I hear it's a great book, didn't want you to miss it" on the inside of the first page. I wanted to tell my mother about Ahmer, especially to ward off discussions about how fabulous Zain was, but before I embarked on that discussion, I wanted to clear whatever it was that stood in the air between Ahmer and me like a thick, black cloud. Would that cloud be carried away by the wind, leaving behind a clear, limitless sky? Or would it burst, creating waters deep enough to drown me in a bottomless sea?

The flight seemed longer than usual. Every time I drifted off to sleep, I had vivid dreams, sometimes of red roses in beautiful gardens and other times of loud thunder in a stormy sky. I wanted to feel pure bliss, but questions in my mind continued to pull me away from it. My anxiety added to the usual heaviness I felt in my legs after the long flight.

Two days after I arrived in Pakistan, Sara rushed into my room with a giggle and told me that we were expecting a guest for tea that evening.

"Who?" I said, trying to readapt to the constant influx of guests at all times of the day.

"Lubna Aunty is coming over. She is dying to meet you," Sara said, still giggling uncontrollably like girls her age frequently did.

"Who?" I repeated, unable to recollect any acquaintance by that name.

"Zain Bhai's mother," she said.

I was appalled by this news. I could not believe that my mother was going ahead with this without discussing it with me. I had just arrived, it had taken two days to get my sleep-wake cycle straight, and now she was already planning my wedding. I was not going to marry Zain, and the sooner he and his family were informed of this, the better it would be for everybody. I silently prayed for Ahmer to arrive before I was forced to create a scene at home. I was anxious to make our bond official and final, so I could explain my reservations about meeting Zain.

"Please, Sara," I said, trying not to be angry with her. "Why are you calling him Zain Bhai? He is not your relative."

"Not yet, not yet," she replied, still laughing.

I could not comprehend why my mother had decided that I was going to say yes and had felt confident enough to involve Sara in this conspiracy. Ammi came into my room that afternoon with a thoroughly pressed green *shalwar kameez*. "Blow-dry your hair so it looks proper," she said. "She will be here by five o'clock."

"Ammi, I really can't. I need to talk to you about—"

"Please. Do this much for me. It's not like we are fixing a wedding date or anything. Just meet her. She has been waiting for a long time to see you and talk to you. You kept putting off your visit, but she was still patient and didn't go around looking for other matches. We owe her this much courtesy at least. She is just coming by herself. We will have tea, that's all."

Before I knew it, I found myself in the midst of a not-so-uncommon scenario. The mother coming by herself for the screening, enjoying an assortment of mouthwatering *samosas* and other snacks, so if she felt the girl was not good enough, her dear son's time would not have to be wasted. The mothers and sometimes their sons rejected countless girls. How terrible they must feel, to be rejected, I thought, but my fear was different; I was scared to death of being accepted.

I grudgingly dressed up enough to look civil and decent without appearing desperate. I had only agreed to sit for a short while, because Sahir was returning from his dorm and I wanted to chat with him. I wondered what he had to say about this whole situation. Lubna Aunty was a nice lady and thankfully did not bombard me with a list of superficial questions. I was polite and reserved. Before leaving, she asked my mother when she could come over again with her husband and Zain. Unfortunately I had passed the screening.

My mother seemed delighted that I had not said anything offensive or bold and that I had not behaved overly modern or Americanized. She invited them over for dinner the following weekend, but she said Zain would be out of town, and right after, we were moving, so a pact was made to finalize the dinner over the phone. Thankfully that would be well after Ahmer's arrival. I had to sort everything out before then. Whatever Ahmer had to tell me, I was sure it would not change my answer. But I still had to gather the courage to tell Ammi about it and deal with the reaction of my stepfather, who was bound to create difficulties. I had to have a backup plan in case things did not work out in the predicted fashion. My plan, inspired by what I had seen in movies, was to take Zain into confidence and beg him to reject me. I would tell him that I was interested in someone else and hope that he would not feel the obligation to share this information with his mother, who would undoubtedly feel the obligation to share it with the rest of town.

Before I knew it, Ahmer had arrived in Karachi. I informed him about the meeting with Lubna Aunty. I told him she was wonderful and that Sara had told me that "Zain Bhai" was extremely good-looking. He laughed for several minutes. I was trying to make him jealous, and he was enjoying the humor in all of this. But in my heart I was thinking, my life is on the line. It's all funny right now, but it won't be if my mother says yes and I end up in the difficult situation of having to rebel against her once again. I did not want to waste any time, and the uncertainty was creating ulcers in the pit of my stomach. The following day he picked me up, taking me to an unknown destination to meet the person he had promised to introduce me to. I was afraid someone would see us.

"Imagine if Zain's mother saw us together," I said, frantic with worry. "Or my stepfather."

"Don't worry," Ahmer replied. "We will be back soon." He looked serious, and the jovial smile on his face had evaporated.

I could not take the suspense any longer and suddenly asked, "Are you married, Ahmer? Please tell me you are not married and you don't have a child. I have thought about these possibilities, but please tell me now. I need to know."

He appeared flabbergasted. "What? Married? Children? What are you saying, Sana? If you thought that was my secret, you don't know me at all, and I am utterly disappointed. I would never have loved you or proposed to you if I was married. You have known me for so long. What are you saying?"

"I'm sorry. I knew I shouldn't jump to conclusions, but I was just so worried about losing you, that's all. I am relieved. What is your secret then? What could it possibly be?"

He paused for a minute, and I saw the faraway look in his eyes once again. It was a look of agony and of having endured; the look of a troubled past and an uncertain future. "What I have hidden from you is not anything to do with us. It's only to do with me and who I am."

My mind started racing from one unbelievable thought to another. Was he a spy? A terrorist? He had changed his 9/11 travel plans, had he not? Had he known something about them? He had given me a lot of information about the hijackers while critiquing my writing. As these questions arose, I knew I was being ridiculous. Working on my thesis had made me such a suspicious person. The jetlag and Zain's mother showing up had added to my paranoia. I was doubting the veracity and sincerity of the one I trusted and cared for the most. The thought of losing Ahmer was so unbearable to me that I was losing my mind. I inhaled deeply and said a prayer in my heart, waiting to hear the truth.

"My father is not dead, Sana."

I breathed a sigh of relief. This was shocking, but it was certainly a shock far more welcome than what my delusional mind had begun to fear. "What? That was your secret? That is wonderful to know. I cannot believe you didn't tell me. We've known each other for years, and all this time I thought you were an orphan. Why did you hide that from me? To gain my sympathy?"

"No. It's not that at all. I'm sorry. He is alive but not really. He has been separated from me just as much as your father has been separated from you. He is in prison, serving a life sentence. I want you to meet him. You always asked me why I became a lawyer. It was so that I could reopen his case and appeal to the Supreme Court."

"What is he in prison for?"

"First-degree murder."

I was both surprised and deeply hurt that Ahmer had kept such a big secret from me. "Why didn't you tell me this before?"

"Because the moment I met you, I knew you were the one for me, Sana. I knew from the first day, the first moment, when you were holding Pride and Prejudice that I wanted to marry you. I had never met anyone like you before. If I told you I was the son of a convicted killer, it would have driven you away from me. You are a person of high morals. This revelation is disturbing you a lot even now, after you in your heart have decided to marry me, isn't it?"

"I cannot say it isn't. It is bothering me a lot but not enough to change my decision."

"I wanted you to know before you said yes."

"How long has he been in prison?"

"Sixteen years."

"Oh my God, that must have been so hard for you."

"Yes. That night of February 11, 1987 changed my life."

I felt a chill go through my spine. I felt an earthquake of a high magnitude shaking my core from within. "Whose murder is he charged with?" I asked, not sure if I could brace myself to hear the answer.

"That doesn't matter. What matters is—"

"Believe me, it matters a lot. It's night and day. It's life or death. It's yes or no to your marriage proposal."

"Asad Shah."

I wished for the ground to open and swallow me up. I could not believe that he had uttered my father's name. A blend of shock, disbelief, and sorrow overcame me. I could not comprehend how this could be happening, that my fairy tale was crumbling before it had concluded. Did I not deserve to be happy? Now I understood what Jennifer had often said: If something seems too good to be true, it probably is.

I loved Ahmer. I cared for him like I had cared for no one before. I understood him. He had taught me to smile again. But now it was all gone. How could I have fallen in love with the son of my father's killer? Was he the only man in the world I could find? How coincidental it all was. We had met on February 11, when I had been mourning my father's death and Ahmer had likely been mourning what had led to his father's imprisonment. I found myself in a predicament that I never could have foreseen. Certainly, no matter how much I loved him, I could not marry him. How could I wake up next to him every morning, look into his eyes, and not see his father's evil? How could I take up the name of those who had destroyed my family? How could I bear my children's grandfather being my sworn lifelong enemy? I could not. I would not.

Had I not removed the picture from my wallet to give to Sara, I would have shown it to Ahmer. Had I not moved all the photographs on the wall in the sitting room in my apartment, he might have seen the picture. Maybe if I had met the killer in person, I would have known about Ahmer being his son. Ahmer's last name, Khan, was the most common last name in the country, so it had not seemed conspicuous to me at all. Maybe if I had told Ahmer about myself and who my father was, neither of us would have invested our emotions to this extent. I had loved deeply and honestly. I had loved with every chamber of my heart. I had given my soul and devoted my life to the wrong man.

By then my face was buried in my hands and I was crying inconsolably. "I have to go," I said, my voice shaking. "I have to get out of the car now."

"What's wrong?" Ahmer said, his voice filled with concern and surprise.

"What's wrong is that your secret and my secret are the same. What I didn't tell you was who my father was and how he died. He was killed the night of February 11, 1987. He was Asad Shah."

"How can that be? Your last name is Rehman."

"That's a gift from my stepfather. He adopted us officially, remember?"

"Sana, listen to me."

"Ahmer, your father has ruined my life. I thought I had found a new life because of you, but you are his son. You cannot change your name; you cannot change your DNA. I don't want to ever see you again. I have spent my whole life hating your father, wishing the worst for him and his family. I cannot marry you."

He refused to leave me in the middle of the road, and insisted on dropping me home. We rode in silence, our minds speaking a thousand words. This was after I had spent the last few weeks planning how I would say yes, and envisioning every color of the rainbow that my life would become. I had gone far to escape my dark past and fate had brought me back to where my misery had been born. I had been feeling like a peak of a mountain, a star in the sky. The mountain had caved and the star had fallen. My fairytale had disintegrated, bringing my beautiful dream to an abrupt end. In a moment, my whole life was turned upside down—all over again.

Chapter 14

A week went by, and I isolated myself completely, spending my time silently brooding over my ruined future within the confines of my bedroom. I gazed at the ceiling fan as it continued to obediently stir the air above my head. I stared at the wall, eyeing the clock that seemed to be looking back at me, mocking me. The seconds hand seemed to be dancing as it moved, as though it were relishing in the joke that time had played on me. Solitude became my new friend. I listened to *ghazals* constantly to try to ward off the silence that was engulfing me. I did not feel the usual compulsion to sing along. I merely listened, allowing the poetic words to become verbose companions to my silent sorrow. I listened to Abida Parveen's *ghazals* by Faiz, poetry that Ahmer had himself explained to me so diligently, not knowing then how well I would understand the essence of those words years later:

> *Ask not about the eve of separation*
> *It came and passed by,*
> *The heart once again cheered up,*
> *Life once again steadied itself.*

Ahmer had explained that even though Faiz was trivializing the experience of being separated from his beloved, the reader could feel his deep sense of loss.

> *When I remembered you*
> *The morning became fragrant*
> *When I awoke my sorrow for you*
> *The night grew restless.*

I retrieved Faiz's book, which I had taken with me, and read the lines while I listened intently. I placed my finger on the rose petals that this book of poetry had preserved for me so beautifully. An unchecked tear rolled down my cheek onto the book, touching the verse I was reading, soaking the shriveled petal that had separated itself from the rest of the flower. I adjusted the volume to the highest setting so I could shut out the sound of the crows at my window. But there was no volume loud enough to overpower the voice of Ahmer, which continued to ring in my ears. He was everywhere—in the books I read, in the words I wrote, in the music I listened to.

I needed to get accustomed to this new and tragic chapter of my life without Ahmer. But how was I to forget him? He was not a dream that could disappear before the beginning of the next day, he was a six year long reality. He was not a word that could be erased or a phrase that could be edited; he was my whole story.

I felt empty and worthless, like a forgotten suitcase in an old closet. My mother was appropriately worried about me. I had told her that I wanted to share something with her and that I had never been more happy in my life. And now I had become the epitome of grief. My eyes were always swollen from crying, and I never smiled. I spent most of my time in my room, immersing myself in my books. I made myself part of every story so I could forget my own. I continued to work on my 9/11 documentary, editing out all that seemed redundant. Only Ahmer could have given me the feedback I needed to smooth out the rough edges and to make everything come together and fall perfectly into place. But he was gone.

My misfortunes had hardened me, yet they had failed to strengthen me. Instead they had made me brittle, and I felt broken into a thousand pieces. I had not spoken to Ahmer, although he had been quite persistent and continued to call and e-mail me. The bitter, angry, and rebellious person within me had reemerged, and reconciliation did not seem feasible. I deleted his e-mails without reading them and erased his messages without hearing them—all except the first one.

"I will always love you, Sana. You are the best thing that ever happened to me, and I will be right here waiting for you," he had said.

I saved it and listened to it sometimes, shedding endless tears over my lost love. It was not his fault whose son he was, but he had hidden the truth from me, and that had cost us both so much. The truth was more valuable to me than the most exquisite jewel. My father had always attached so much emphasis to the truth and had so rightly opposed covering up the truth. Hadn't those been Ahmer's own sentiments? Truth had been important to Ahmer, but perhaps not as much as it had been to me. I had spent six years of my life loving the wrong person. If I had known the truth about him, I would never have spoken a single word to him. Perhaps he was just like his mother in character as he was in appearance; perhaps he hadn't inherited his father's evil. But no matter how I looked at it, the picture was bleak, and making things work out between us seemed impossible.

After reliving all our memorable moments and mourning the tragic ending of our love story, I realized that it was not fair to my family to see me withering away. I decided to tell my mother that I was willing to marry Zain. It would be no less than a self-inflicted punishment, but maybe that would be my atonement and my mother's compensation for what she had endured on my account. I could not love again. But I needed to live again. In order to do that I had to do what I should have done years ago: meet the person who had ruined my past and, in a peculiar twist of fate, ruined my future as well.

My hatred for him had mushroomed over the past few days. I would go to meet him, but I would have to do it discreetly, without involving anyone else. I had been thinking about this since I was nine years old. I had to see him, look into his evil green eyes, and ask him why he had, for things and money, taken away my entire universe. I needed to remind him that he had taken away a little girl's smile, and replaced it with cries of deep sorrow. How would he know if I didn't tell him, that years later, that horrible moment still came to haunt me every night and stayed with me every waking hour.

The drive to the prison was long and the roads were unusually deserted. Gray clouds blanketed the sky. I felt my hands shaking and my heart skipping several beats as I got closer. I felt cold on this hot summer day. I felt giddy from the humidity as well as my lack of sleep and exhausted from the plethora of thoughts running through my mind. I had covered myself with a large white scarf—a *chaadar*. I was afraid to enter the high-security prison unaccompanied. I did not want to attract any attention and wondered what my mother would think about my daring move. I was sure she would disapprove vehemently and declare it unsafe for a girl to go alone to such places. That was why I had not taken her into confidence; this was something I had to do alone. My alibi was that I was going to different parts of the city to conduct interviews for my documentary, which I had been working on. My mother had opposed that idea as well, due to safety issues, but had ultimately given her reluctant permission.

As I approached, I saw two guardsmen standing on either side of the black prison gate in perfect symmetry. Their khaki uniforms camouflaged them effectively, so they appeared to be part of the brown walls adjacent to the gate; if it were not for the rifles slung across their shoulders, they could easily be completely invisible.

It was a long walk across a large expanse of land that had occasional patches of grass burnt yellow by the sun. The fields were surrounded by silver fences that were mostly coated with rust and topped with coils of barbed wire. It started to drizzle, and not having an umbrella, I was grateful for having the *chaa-*

dar and used it as my shield against the unexpected weather. Through the fence, I saw a group of uniformed inmates marching and singing a patriotic song in unison, *"Ai Watan Kay Sajeelay Javaanon"* (O brave soldiers of the nation), an old classic by Noor Jehan. A bird hummed a sad tune on a breaking branch of a weeping willow.

After being cleared through security, parting with my cell phone, and taking several deep breaths, I walked slowly through the dimly lit corridors. The walls were covered with yellow paint that was peeling off and decorated by graffiti that had been penned by countless inmates over the years. Patches marked the ceiling where water had leaked in monsoons gone by. Even now, there were several buckets lined up to collect water from the day's downpour. My shoes made a splashing sound as they hit the wet floor. From the corner of my eye I saw an aged prisoner with a white beard and long white hair crouched in a corner mumbling inaudible words; he seemed to have lost his mind. Somewhere in the distance there appeared to be a commotion related to an internal dispute that was breaking out among the inmates. As I continued my walk into the high-security area, a deafening silence ensued. I felt frightened by the realization that I was amidst the worst form of humanity. The portion of the prison that I was walking through housed people who had killed in cold blood. The air felt thick, as though it were carrying the heavy burden of sin.

I had been granted fifteen minutes for this meeting, and Shehryar Khan had been informed of my arrival. How would I be able to tell him everything I had planned to tell him for more than fifteen years in fifteen minutes? How would I convey in a brief, timed conversation, the sorrow of a lifetime? But the moment I had been waiting for had finally arrived. I wondered how I would feel after the meeting. Would it give me some relief and some closure, or would it simply reinforce my anger and make my wounds raw again? For a minute I hesitated and considered retracing my steps. But that would make me a coward who could not face her fears. I knew this was going to be difficult, but I also knew that if I did not go through with this, I might regret it for the rest of my life. Maybe that was why fate had brought me to Ahmer—so I would stop procrastinating and finally face the harsh reality of my father's murder.

A thin policeman in a navy-blue uniform greeted me. His manner was cold, and his voice was punctuated with irritation as he escorted me to the cell. He seemed both annoyed and amused that a woman had interrupted his important schedule.

"This is Shehryar Khan," he scornfully mumbled, leaving us to talk through the metal bars. I had promised myself I would not cry, break down, or show any sign of weakness. This was not like a college presentation I had practiced for a few days; this was the centerpiece of my life. This was the meeting I had dreamed of for sixteen years. I had been rehearsing it since I was a child. Yet I had delayed it, hiding behind a shield of sorrow, and my affliction had grown. I would say what I was there to say, release the venom that was within me, and leave immediately after, without giving him a chance to beg for mercy. I was afraid of what he might say if I gave him the chance. Would he try to defend such a crime? Would he try to justify killing my father for money and a watch, claiming that he was poor and needed to feed or educate his family?

I felt my lips tremble and was unable to look at him right away. I stared at the mosaic patterns on the floor. I looked at the fly that buzzed aimlessly from one side to another. I gazed at the decades-old gray clock that reminded me that only fourteen minutes remained. I was face-to-face with my enemy and was prepared to make the most important speech of my life. I hoped that I would walk out of this prison cell with my head held high and the weapon to eradicate my sorrow finally within my reach.

"Ahmer has told me so much about you," he said, startling me. "I was expecting both of you to come together, but I am so happy to see you, Sana. Ahmer has said such wonderful things about you."

I had heard his voice; he had said my name. It made me shudder. I still could not muster the courage to look at him. "We are not getting married," I said coolly. "Asad Shah was my father."

It came out as a plain and simple fact, clean and sharp as the edge of a new razor blade. And then I looked up. Standing before me was a man who appeared defeated, a man who had suffered and lost. His prisoner uniform hung loosely from his thin frame. He was a man who had grown old before his time, who had lived through great pain and misery. His hair was an unevenly trimmed mass of gray, as was the stubble that covered his chin. Through it I could still see the barely visible dimple that he had passed on to Ahmer in its exact form. And then I looked at his eyes. Their lids seemed heavy from having carried the weight of sorrow, exhausted from years of looking at metal bars and unchanging walls. They appeared weathered from endless tears that had soaked their edges. I looked again to be sure. They were kind and forgiving. Yes indeed. They were generous and caring. They were listless and lifeless. But most importantly, they were the darkest shade of brown.

Chapter 15

In an instant, I felt all the blood inside my body rush to the bottom of my feet. The bars behind which Shehryar Khan stood blended into one another as everything seemed to swirl around me. I felt as though I was standing on quicksand that was sucking me in. Before I could bring myself to speak, I turned around and ran. All the words I had rehearsed went up in smoke. The floor was wet from the rain, and I lost my footing and fell. It was a minor fall, but inside I had fallen to the deepest crevice in the ground. My shoe had come off, and my ankle was sprained and aching. I slowly steadied myself, put my shoe back on, and walked out with my head bowed lower than that of the worst prisoner I was leaving behind. In the background, I could still hear the old hunched man talking to himself. He was banging his head against the hard surface of his prison cell. My throat felt dry, and my hands felt cold and numb. The air felt even thicker, and it seemed impossible to breathe.

They had the wrong man. The wrong person was in prison for my father's murder and had been there not for a few days, or months, but for sixteen long years. This had been the meeting I had been anxiously awaiting for more than half my life, hoping to bring closure to this awful tragedy. Instead I was faced with the revelation that an innocent man was behind bars for no fault of his own and the real killer had gone free. How could I have never questioned the authenticity of the investigation? I was a child, but how could none of my family members have known? I, the truth seeker, had hidden the truth about what I had seen, and so many lives had been destroyed as a result. Had I listened to Papa's advice, his last words, his last pearl—silence can be golden, but it is as bad as lying if it is used to hide the truth—this never would have happened. If only I had told someone what I had seen and simply described the face of the man outside the window, I would not be here today. I would not be feeling trapped in an armor of my own guilt or feeling suffocated by the thick smoke of a truth left untold. It was as if Papa had known the future, as if his sixth sense had come forth in those last hours, letting him know how limited his time was and how urgent it was to share his wisdom.

In a way, the words my father had spoken on the last day of his life would have given him justice in death, if only I had listened. I wish I had held on to his words more tightly than all the grudges in my heart. If only I had understood and remembered his advice more clearly than every lecture at Stanford. If only I had not carelessly let that last pearl fall from my clumsy hands. If only I had put the seashell to my ear and heard the ocean, rather than putting it away in a jar of worthless collectables, Shehryar Khan would be a free man. I limped slowly toward the car, wincing a little, and drove home.

The wind was gaining momentum, and the rain was pouring undeterred, slamming uninterrupted against the windows. It was as though the sky were shedding a thousand tears. This innocent man who stood behind iron bars had not seen the light of day for a decade and a half simply because I had kept silent. He had not been there to raise his son. He had not been at his wife's bedside when she had died a painful death. He had lost everything, all because of a girl who had decided to bury the past. Had I told someone what I had seen, the right person might have been behind bars today and this innocent man might have been spared a life of incarceration. He might have been free to raise his son, free to see the world, free from the permanent impact of a ruined reputation and liberated from questions of 'what if' and 'what could have been.'

I remembered my father once talking about a man who had been wrongly accused of a crime and later vindicated, saying, "A ruined reputation is like a broken mirror: it can be repaired, but the crack always remains." My father had been proud of me. If he knew the damage my secrecy had caused, his spirit would feel pure agony. He had said I would do great things. Instead, not only had I failed myself, but I had also profoundly failed my father.

The gentleman who had stood helplessly imprisoned across from me had not ruined my life at all. On the contrary, I had ruined his. And here I was, attempting to excel in a career in investigative journalism. I studied about finding the facts and seeking the truth. Never go by what's on the surface. Always dig deeper. Dig until you find the truth. Hadn't those been the words of my learned professor? And I had never questioned the legitimacy of this conviction in a country where corruption was rampant and accountability nonexistent. How could I have been so naïve? Countless times I had thought of meeting this man to confront him but had simply not followed through. I felt like a complete failure. Not only was an innocent man behind bars because of me, but a murderer was free. The little solace I had felt all these years knowing that my father's killer had at least been punished, that he had spent several years behind bars, that he had suffered and repented what he had done, was reduced to nothing. He may have committed more crimes, killed more people, and ruined more lives. Was I to blame for those as well? He was not the prisoner, I was; a prisoner isolated from the world, from those I loved as a consequence of my actions.

My thoughts raced as I questioned who the real killer was. Who was he and where was he? The man who I had spent more than half my life hating, the man whose face was more vivid in my memory than the sequence of the alphabet? I did not know and feared I never would.

I thought about Ahmer and how he had given a new meaning to every dimension of my life. He had understood me like no one else had and had made me realize that despite having experienced tragedy at such an early age, I still had so much to be grateful for. He had truly made me realize that life was a gift to be cherished and to be lived to the fullest. Looking back, I realized that I could have been killed that day if the assassin had seen me. This life was very precious indeed, and I could not waste it wrapped up in bitterness and self-pity. He had brought me closer to my mother and brother, because everything he said had made so much sense to me. I had finally been able to forgive my mother and look beyond the anger I had felt over her second marriage. I was able to at least cross part of the bridge that years of separation had built between my family and me, and it was all because of Ahmer. And what had I done to him and his family? I had put bars of steel between his father and him, which neither of them could break. I had created grounds between them, which neither of them could cross. His father had spent years of his life in a cell that was smaller than my closet.

Ahmer had made me see the good in everyone, including myself. I had evolved from a quiet, introverted girl into a self-confident, cheerful, likable person who had achieved apparent success in every sphere of life. Most of who I had become I owed to Ahmer. He had taken the bitterness from inside me and turned it into sugar. I had been a rock, hard and impenetrable to light, and he had transformed me into a prism, clear and beautiful, one that could allow an entire spectrum of colors to pass through it. Ahmer had given me a new life, not knowing that I was the one who had taken his away.

He had always been so elusive about his past and was such an avid listener that I did not realize how little he had really told me about himself. I always poured my heart out to him, leaving out nothing but the details of my father's demise. He spoke volumes about his mother but seldom mentioned his father. His frequent trips to Pakistan, he said, were to visit his ailing aunt, who had also been diagnosed with breast cancer. It seemed a good enough reason for him to go frequently, so I had never questioned him. Little had I known that although his aunt was a major reason for those visits, his imprisoned father had been the stronger pull. Now I understood the faraway look, the shadow that often darkened his face, the one look that was like a single word from another language that I simply could not read.

I wondered what Ahmer must have gone through when his father was arrested—the pain, the hurt, the humiliation. He may have been present when his father was unjustly put in handcuffs and dragged heartlessly away. I wondered how he must have felt about not being able to hold his father's hand or share stories with him about his days at school or his cricket matches. He must have longed for his father's support during his mother's prolonged illness and painful death. He had likely hoped against hope that one day his father's sentence would be overturned and prayed that someone who knew the truth would come forward. That was what his whole life had probably been about: becoming a lawyer to prove his father's innocence and to have him absolved of a crime he had not committed. What if he had been tormented all his life by the question of whether his father was indeed innocent? The thought of his hurt and what would go through his mind when he found out the truth filled my eyes with tears.

I looked down at my hand and the gold ring I had placed on my finger when I returned home. I slipped it off and placed it on the dresser, realizing that I did not deserve to wear it. What had I done? God had saved Ahmer's life for me, but I had pushed him away and lost him all over again. I did not want anyone at home to know what was going on in my life just yet. I knew my mother and Sara would notice, and since it was all so complicated, I would not know where to begin. I had to get out of the house. Everyone was accustomed to my unpredictable actions by then, so I was rarely questioned about my whereabouts, although my mother was always frantic with worry.

By late afternoon, there was no hint of the heavy rain that had fallen earlier that day, except the muddy puddles on the uneven streets. I drove to the beach that evening to collect my thoughts, to mourn my lost integrity, and to appease the storm that was brewing inside me. The waves of the ocean had always been able to bring about a sense of peace in me. I descended the rocks with some difficulty, owing to my sprained ankle, and sat on the sand gazing at the sky and watching the sun go down, slowly and silently. Hues of red and gold appeared before me, blending in smoothly like watercolors on a canvas. The clouds were low and stood out against the clear sky, like the finest strokes of a paintbrush. The tide was high, and the sea was unpredictably rough, a flawless reenactment of the turmoil I had experienced earlier that day. The turbulent waves were interrupted by rocks that lay in their path, becoming calmer, gentler, and more beautiful as they retreated. For the turbulence in my life, Ahmer had been my rock, and now that rock was gone. He had been like the dam that stood unflinching between a dreadful storm and me. Now there was nothing to stop the turmoil and no one to halt the water flowing from the high tide. I witnessed the evening dissolve into a dark, starless night.

I drove home, listening to the Faiz by Abida CD in my car.

If the destination is concealed from view, let the quest be
If reunion is not attainable, let the longing be
If waiting is too tedious, then in the meanwhile, O' heart
On someone's promise of tomorrow, let conversation be.

When I reached home, I went to my room, buried my face in my hands, and sobbed, just like the nine-year-old girl had on that night in 1987.

Chapter 16

I woke up the next morning with my head pounding so hard I thought it would explode. I had spent nearly all night awake, trying in vain to bring a pause to the devastation inside me. I had barely fallen asleep when my dream returned; in this one, there was blood and I was trying to escape, but this time my ankle was bound by a rusted silver metal chain. When I tried to move, I was unable to break free. Every time I tried to loosen the chain, I heard the loud clanking of metal, and in the dream, the sound became progressively louder until I was jolted awake. As the *Fajr Azaan* approached my ears, I realized I was perspiring, and my ankle hurt when I tried to get out of bed. I had not slept well in years, often tossing and turning restlessly in bed, thinking of the past and struggling to find peace. But this was a new kind of insomnia.

I had always read stories about how the guilt of a bad deed could torment a person and how remorse could take over and destroy a whole life. I thought of Mr. DeWinters in *Rebecca,* and Amir in *The Kite Runner.* But it was now that I truly experienced the stab of a tarnished conscience and deeply felt the weight of guilt. I had turned in bed for hours, my feet bathing in sparkling sateen sheets, my head embedded in a soft down pillow, the cool air of the air conditioner blowing in my face. All night I thought of Ahmer's father, whose bed was a concrete floor in a hot prison cell, his food a meager consortium of lentils and onions, and his companions cruel policemen who spat in his face. In a place where spending an hour would be hard to bear, he had spent sixteen long years.

I remembered the time long ago, in second grade, when I had been punished for talking too much in class. I had not been talking but happened to have been sitting next to the girls making noise, and I had been erroneously included in the punishment. The crime had been minor, and the penalty was that I had to write one hundred times "I will not make noise during class again." Nevertheless, every word of those one hundred lines had been painful to write. My encounter with a false allegation had been brief and superficial, with the only consequence perhaps being an improvement in my handwriting. Yet so many years later, I still remembered how terrible it had made me feel. I could not imagine what feelings a false accusation of murder must have evoked.

I swallowed two Tylenols with a cup of hot tea, hoping they would relieve my headache if not my ankle pain, and started figuring out what to do next. This secret could not remain undisclosed any longer; the truth had to be told. I was not going to hold any false hopes about Ahmer. I had to accept the fact that our friendship would have to become my cherished memory. Ahmer would always be a part of me, and I would never cease caring for him. But there was no way we could build a life together on the backdrop of such a tainted past. Even with the most harmonious colors, a beautiful painting could not emerge on a ruined canvas.

I knew that regardless of all the obstacles, I had to get his father out of prison. I wondered what—if any—connection he had with my father and why he had confessed to a murder he had not committed. I was not going to entertain any unrealistic expectations of ever being able to learn who had taken my father's life; that only happened in books and movies. In reality, countless criminals remained unpunished in this life. We lived in a world of injustice. I could not take away the pain and suffering that sixteen years of incarceration had caused Ahmer's father, but I also could not live in peace if I did not get him out of there soon. I was accountable for every single minute he was spending in jail now. I knew he was not the killer, but who would believe me? Who would believe the testimony of a witness who was only nine years old at the time of the crime? Who would believe me after sixteen years had elapsed? And who would believe it if they found out the connection I had with Ahmer? I had no proof; I only had a picture in my mind, which was clearer than crystal but which tragically no one else could see.

Regardless of these difficulties, I owed Ahmer and his father the truth. If Ammi took my word for it, we would at least be able to have Shehryar Khan exonerated on grounds of mercy and pardon. I had to confide in my mother or Phuppo. My aunt was far away, but I talked to her often over the telephone. Owing to the innovative technology of Internet and calling cards, long distances no longer seemed that far. I had told her about Ahmer before, carefully deleting the part about the proposal and disclosing only that I had met someone and would tell her more soon. She had been comforted to see me happy but understandably apprehensive about my choice. However, I had been confident of her approval, which was as important to me, if not more so than my mother's.

I called Phuppo, because I thought she might be able to guide me, and give me sound advice regarding the optimal strategy to break this news to my mother. She was not home, so I hung up without leaving a message. As I was putting my thoughts together, I left my room and walked into the sitting room. I saw my mother seated on the floor amidst countless brown cardboard boxes. The sight and smell of them took me back several years to the time that our home had fallen apart. Brown boxes had become a symbol of something being taken away, pieces of me, bit by bit, and their smell made me nauseous to this day. There were still a few weeks remaining before the final move, but the tedious process of categorizing and discarding had begun. It would help get my mind off things, I thought, even though I had to face them and conquer them, rather than putting them away with the miscellaneous boxes. Procrastination, which had cost me so much, could no longer be my way of life.

I offered to pick Sara up from school, and on the way she asked me what was wrong with me. I told her I had not slept well and had a headache as a result.

After lunch we all busied ourselves with packing and organizing. "Are you OK, dear?" my mother asked perceptively.

Even though we had lived apart, she knew me inside out, and it was impossible to hide my misery from her.

"Why are you limping?" she asked, observing my foot.

"I sprained my ankle, so it hurts to put weight on it." She immediately applied some nonsteroidal cream and bandaged it.

"How did you sprain it? Were you running after people to beg them for interviews? You should be careful. Anyway I don't like the idea of your going to strange parts of town by yourself."

"Don't worry about me so much. I have other crew members with me when we are shooting. You know how passionate I am about this project."

"I know how passionate you are but don't expect me not to worry."

"Thank you, that feels good, Ammi," I said, as I put my bandaged foot up on the couch.

"Please don't thank me, Sana. You will never know how I felt whenever you got sick and I was so far away. When you had the chicken pox, when you had fevers, when you went to the dentist—it was so hard not to be there for you during those times to hold your hand and tell you that everything will be fine." She suddenly appeared overcome with emotion and said, "You even have a mark of a cut on the sole of your foot, that I didn't even know about."

"Yeah, I stepped on broken glass two years ago. It was a small cut, really."

"You seemed so happy and you told me about some good news to wait for, and now your face is swollen like you have been crying a lot. What's wrong?"

"I'll be all right, Ammi, There is something I need to tell you, but I don't know where to start."

"I think you can start with the ring on your dresser, that I just saw this morning. What is the meaning of that? Are you engaged?"

"Come on, Ammi. If I was, I would have told you."

"Then what is a gold ring doing on your dresser? It's a very traditional ring, made many years ago, I'm sure. And I have never seen you buy jewelry for yourself."

"I was going to be engaged. That's why the ring is there. There would have been an engagement only after a formal proposal, and I would have accepted it if it had been OK with you and your husband and Phuppo and Phuppa."

"So when do we get to see him?" Her face had a hint of a smile at the thought that her daughter was grown up enough to step into matrimony, blended in with a disappointment that it might not be with Zain.

"It's all over, Ammi. There won't be an engagement. I will explain everything, but there is something more important—"

"I never wanted you to get hurt, Sana. That's how boys are these days. They are not sincere, and when you are so young and in love, you do not understand those things. I didn't want to put restrictions on you because I felt I didn't have the right, and now your heart is broken."

"No, Ammi, it's not at all what you think. He didn't break my heart. He has already asked me to marry him. I am the one to blame. He is a wonderful person. He is the one who made me realize the value of my family. The girl he marries will be lucky to have him. But it can never be me, and it's all my fault." I felt tears well up in my eyes once again and struggled to hold them back.

"Sana, if you tell me, maybe I can help you. If you don't feel comfortable talking to me, perhaps you can call Phuppo; I'm sure she will give you some good advice, and this can all be sorted out."

"Ammi, please let's work on some boxes and clear some shelves. It's over for good." I wanted to tell her about Shehryar Khan. It would take courage for me to bring up what had been buried for so many years, but I was desperate to unburden myself, yet I could tell her only if she dropped the subject of my engagement.

"Then promise me you will think about Zain. I have to give his mother an answer soon."

I could not believe my mother was bringing another man's name into the conversation when she could see that I was in the middle of an emotional crisis. But in the back of my mind, I was already thinking that marriage would be the best way to bid farewell to Ahmer for good. If I married someone else, Ahmer, the honorable person that he was, would leave me alone. It might make it easier for him to forget me if he could despise me. But could I betray him? Could I betray myself? Was it fair to the person I would marry to profess my love and devotion to him when I had already promised my heart to another? Yes, of course it was. Wasn't all fair in love and war?

"I don't need to think about it. You can say yes to Zain's mother," I said rather sharply.

"I have wanted to hear a yes from you, Sana, but not like this. I wanted to hear a happy yes, not a yes as a rebound from whatever it is you are rebounding from."

"How can I give a happy yes for a person I haven't met in my life? Things happen, Ammi. When you married Papa, you never imagined you would be married to someone else. But you are, aren't you? All love stories are not meant to be forever."

My bottled up frustration about having to hold on to my secret had angered me, and I had ended up upsetting my mother as well as myself to a point that discussing Shehryar Khan at that moment had become impossible.

"Please don't bring me into this. We are talking about you. I am just saying that if things haven't worked out with the person you chose then let them work out with the person we have chosen for you. Young people only see love; older people can see beyond that blinding shield. Even if love is true and it is reciprocated, it isn't enough. There is a lot more that a marriage needs for nourishment. If love were enough, there wouldn't be any divorces in the western world."

My mother and I reached an agreement that this was not the most opportune time to discuss this issue and agreed to revisit it at a later time. As for the truth about Ahmer's father, I promised myself that another sun would not set with this secret unshared. We started clearing the storeroom of things that had remained unused for too long. Hours went by, and several stacks of giveaways and innumerable bags of trash emerged. I found some memorabilia that I started placing in a box. My childhood clothes, Sahir's first pair of shoes, and the yellow Winnie-The-Pooh blanket we had brought him home in were among the valuables that had been collected over the years. Sahir wanted to keep one of his old toys, my mother said, pointing to the red fire truck with firemen and a yellow ladder. I remembered it vividly as being the one my father had brought him from his trip to London. I was both surprised and touched that my brother had cherished what little he remembered of Papa.

We proceeded to sort through a boxful of Sara's school projects, from painted handprints she had made in kindergarten to her high school painting of the city life of Karachi, which had won her a national prize. Sara still had so many dolls, and motherly as she was, she could not part with all of them. We could give away her childhood fairy tale books, if nothing else, although I wanted to preserve *Snow White and the Seven Dwarves*.

"What should we do with all these cassettes? I don't even have a cassette player anymore. Everything is on CD now," I said, fondly remembering how Sahir would find a cassette, pull out the tape, and get it all tangled up and how Papa would fix it with a pencil.

"We still have a cassette player and it works, so we should keep them. There are many good oldies that are not on CDs yet," my mother said, so I put them carefully in a box and labeled it before putting it away.

Next, I proceeded to the bookshelf, which I had volunteered to take care of, mainly for selfish reasons. I picked up a few Agatha Christie novels and a handful of Daphne du Maurier books, setting them aside for myself. I pulled out some books by Jane Austen so I could wrap myself in literature. It would be the ideal escape from thoughts of my broken engagement, an impending marriage, an innocent man's incarceration, and my worst enemy's freedom.

"If you are done with the books, I need some help with these albums on the top shelf; they are too high for me to reach," my mother said.

I stretched my arms to reach the top shelf and coughed a little as I inhaled some dust particles. I retrieved a cleaning cloth and as I wiped away what seemed like several layers of grime, many beautiful albums emerged. "These look ancient," I remarked, curious to know if they had any of my father's photographs.

"They are all mixed up, but many of them have old pictures. After we clear some of this mess we can probably take a break and look at these; we can reminisce about old times over some five o'clock tea," my mother suggested.

I welcomed the idea. "I didn't know you still had any pictures of Papa," I said, my voice low.

My mother appeared somewhat defensive. "Of course I do. They are just not on the wall. He will always be part of my life.

I am happily married now but I will never forget your father. He was a great husband and a great father."

This was the first time in so many years that I had heard my mother say anything about him. She was so much more open when my stepfather was not around. I wished she had said these things sixteen years earlier.

Over a cup of hot, flavorful tea, we became engrossed in admiring childhood pictures and talking about the good old days. We dipped our Nice Biscuits in the tea, staying true to tradition. Soon I came across a really old album with my father's pictures from his early days; it had been my grandfather's album. "This must be Phuppo," I said, looking fondly at a childhood picture of my father with his younger sister. They were both sitting in the garden, and Papa was looking at her with admiration. They were eating mangoes, their faces covered in juice and yellow pulp.

"Can I have it?" I said.

"Of course, my dear," Ammi said. "Everything here is yours. You can take whatever you want."

Years ago, seeing my father's photographs had always saddened me. But after Ahmer's influence, I had learned to celebrate my father's life and was able to look at such pictures with a sense of happiness and pride.

We continued to chat about family and life while perusing the albums. Suddenly, as I was casually flipping through the thick pages, sticky at the corners with old glue, observing the bell-bottom style pants and the long side burns of the sixties, a wave of recognition suddenly swept over me. There it was, clearer than my own name: the face of the man I had promised to remember and promised to hate. It was undoubtedly the face of my sworn enemy. It was from his younger days, but I nearly jumped out of my seat as I saw the prominent diagonal scar on his forehead and the unforgettable eyes. The unmistakable emerald eyes of my father's killer were staring back at me from a yellowing page of a forgotten album.

Chapter 17

I had to find out who he was. I knew beyond a shadow of doubt that this was a picture of my father's assassin.

"Who is this?" I blurted out, attempting to conceal the hurricane of emotions within me.

"It's Amjad Bhai, your uncle. He's your dad's half brother."

"How come I never knew of his existence? Where is he? So did Dada [grandpa] have two wives?"

"Yes. Your grandmother was his second wife. It was not uncommon in those days and in this culture to have two wives, one in the village and one in the city. Your father did not like to talk about it much, because the families were not on good terms with one another. There was a rift over land and who should get what after your grandfather's passing. It was so petty that your father did not want to discuss it, and he wanted you and Sahir to be kept as far away from it as possible. There was a time when he tried on his own to patch things up, but his brother did not want to maintain any relationship."

"Where is he now?" I asked, surprised at how the missing pieces of this puzzle seemed to be coming together in such an unexpected fashion.

"I was in touch with him periodically due to property matters, so I know where he lives, but I don't maintain any contact now. There was some controversy about that piece of land— whether you and Sahir would inherit it or Amjad Bhai was entitled to receive it—but I was depressed and under so much stress that I didn't want to take on the additional burden of going to the courts and fighting over it. I thought we already had plenty anyway, and they had probably been deprived, so I let it go."

"So you are saying I would have never known this if I hadn't come across this album?"

"Yes, perhaps."

"I can't believe that Phuppo didn't mention anything for all these years either. She often talked about her childhood and Papa and her parents. I can't believe I didn't know such an important fact."

"Well, you know now," said Ammi, not realizing the impact of this revelation on my psyche.

"I need his address."

"Why, Sana? Please don't. I know you want to hold on in any way possible to whatever was connected to your father, but this is different. They did not care for your father at all. He made your dad's life very difficult."

"I have my reasons, Ammi. "I need the address. This, too, I will explain later."

"I don't understand your mysteries. There is no way you can go there. It's in the middle of the village, and it's a dangerous area with lots of violence these days. Forget it." She was exasperated.

I was desperate. I could not tell her everything just yet. I had to know more. I had to see him face-to-face and confront him. I decided to drop it at that moment.

Later that evening, I snuck in to where I knew important documents were kept. Among the cardboard boxes I had seen one labeled "legal papers and letters." After sifting through several stacks of papers, and shuffling a multitude of files, I came across a large envelope with the name Amjad Shah printed across it. As soon as I found the address, I called up Amna and went over to her house. She knew the interior village areas well and said her driver was quite familiar with the area. I did not explain to her the purpose of my visit but told her that my life depended on it. She offered to accompany me on my journey.

"Shakoor is a good driver and is very reliable. You know that we have had him for almost twenty years. He can take us. If you prefer to go alone, that's fine too. Just tell me what day."

"Is tomorrow morning a possibility?" I asked earnestly.

"Sure," she replied.

Amna was such a dear friend, and whenever I met her after a gap of several years, somehow it never seemed like a long time. We could talk for hours and catch up on all that we had missed out on, filling in all the blanks, and not have to think about what to say next. That was the special bond between childhood friends. I could trust her and I knew she would always be there for me when I needed her. I had so much piled up inside of me that I desperately needed to share it with someone. She had known about Ahmer for a few years, so I decided to tell her that things had not worked out for us. I did not feel ready to share with her the reasons behind our separation.

"I am so sorry things didn't work out," she said with tears in her eyes. I could see that she was feeling my pain.

"You know, a lot is not clear; I am not sure about many things. I will tell you the whole story when I get back."

"That's fine, just don't do anything dangerous. You are too precious to me." She gave me a warm hug and promised me that her car would be there with Shakoor at seven in the morning.

I wanted to leave before everyone woke up and before my plans could be defeated. I scribbled a note that Amna's car had picked me, which was true, and that I would return before sunset. It was comfortably cool in the morning but was slowly warming up to be a hot and humid day. We had to traverse a large expanse of desert, but with Shakoor's expertise in finding shortcuts, we crossed it rather quickly.

I tried to remain calm and fill my mind with happy thoughts, but it seemed an unachievable task. My hatred for Amjad Shah was palpable; not only had he taken my father's life, but he had also let an innocent man take the blame for it. How could he sleep at night, knowing one innocent person was dead and another was locked up in prison? How could he eat a meal knowing someone was nearly starving, imprisoned in a cell from where there was no escape? He had ruined many childhoods. And he was my half uncle; this I had never expected. His father was my very own grandfather. My father had such high moral values, yet his own brother was so full of sin and greed. He had killed Papa for money and land. Could he be happy after committing such a crime? Could all those inconsequential things bring him any joy?

My train of thought was interrupted by a group of beggars knocking at the car window when we stopped at a traffic signal. I quickly gave them some change that I had in my purse. I used to always feel sorry for these poor people, particularly the children who were made to beg on the streets, and angry at the feudals who did not want them to ever receive the gift of education, since that would empower them to fight for their rights. I looked at the youngest of the beggars, who was likely eight or nine years old. He was barefoot, with his face covered in dirt, his hair disheveled, and his shirt riddled with holes. I wondered what his life was like and felt that my problems at this moment paled in comparison to his.

While Shakoor was switching channels on the radio, the word "forgiveness" caught my attention, and I asked him to stay tuned in to that channel. It was a regular program that I had listened to before, with panel discussions about a subject. That day, the topic they had coincidentally chosen was that of revenge and forgiveness. The speaker, who was quoting from the Quran, said, "If thou dost stretch thy hand against me, to slay me, it is not for me to stretch my hand against thee to slay thee: for I do fear God, the cherisher of the worlds [Quran 5:28]."

They went into a discussion about what Allah and the Prophet (peace be upon him) had said about forgiveness, and all the scholars agreed on the fact that the one who forgives is much greater than the one who avenges. They also agreed that punishment was God's right and we should trust him for justice, rather than taking revenge and harboring anger. There was a psychologist on the panel who offered her analysis on forgiveness and said that those who spent their life being vindictive and seeking revenge never found peace and those who found the generosity to forgive and let go gained a new sense of freedom.

I was amazed at the timing of this program being aired at the very moment I was heading to confront my father's murderer. I decided that I was not among those magnanimous souls who had the capability to forgive a sin of such enormity.

We reached the house uneventfully. It was an extremely hot day, and the bright sunlight was almost blinding me as I stood outside the door, waiting for someone to answer. What if nobody was home? I had not even had the phone number to call. What if this was an old address and the person I had come all this way to meet had relocated? I took out a tissue from my purse to wipe the beads of perspiration that had settled on my face and neck. A woman in her sixties opened the door of what appeared to be a modest home in need of significant repair.

"*Salam*. I am here to meet Mr. Amjad Shah." This was the first time I had allowed myself to say his name. "Is he home?"

The woman looked at me kindly but seemed surprised. "He is," she said.

"I am Sana, his brother's daughter." I was gathering by now that this lady was perhaps not the lady of the house.

She showed me the way in and asked me to have a seat. "I will let him know you are here. Would you like some cold *lassi*?" she asked, referring to the traditional refreshing yogurt drink.

"No, thank you," I said, feeling thirsty from the scorching heat but determined not to even have a sip of water in my enemy's home.

She returned after what seemed like a long wait and asked me to go inside to the family room. I started feeling nervous. Maybe he was getting ready with a gun to kill me. Maybe he knew I had seen him that night. Perhaps he was aware that I knew his secret. If I got killed in this desert, no one would ever know. History would repeat itself, the killer would never get caught, and my mother and brother would lose another member of their family. My aunt and uncle would be devastated. I had been so irresponsible. At least when I had gone to meet the supposed killer in prison, there had been metal bars and policemen on duty to protect me. And here I was, alone and unarmed, to meet the real killer and confront him on my own.

What I had done was immature and rash. I could have at least confided in Ahmer; we could have come here together. Then I wondered how he would handle it if something were to happen to me. He might not marry for the rest of his life. But at least he might know one day that I had sacrificed my life trying to sort his out. If I died and the truth came out, it would still be worth it. But if not, it would all be in vain. I wished I had confided in Amna, so at least someone would know. Maybe I would change my stance and just pretend I was here to meet him as an old relative who wanted to patch things up with extended family; then I could return later with the police or Ahmer.

I was jittery and felt cold and weak, like my legs would give way and I would stumble and fall, but I steadied myself and prepared myself once again for this long-awaited moment. I was going to meet my father's killer. I would finally see the evil eyes that had haunted me for sixteen years. I was anticipating a strong, stocky man when suddenly I looked over my shoulder and saw a feeble figure lying on the couch across the room. It was boiling hot, yet he was covered in a blanket. He appeared old and cachectic, his face covered in a graying, untrimmed beard, his gray hair long. His cheeks were hollow and sunken in, and his lips were parched and blistered. He seemed to be in a lot of pain. His eyes closed as he winced and then slowly opened. There they were: the familiar green eyes. I almost jumped at the sight of them. I would have never recognized this man if it had not been for those unmistakable, unforgettable eyes. The diagonal scar on his forehead was visible, as I had remembered, although it was less pronounced. He looked at me with his glassy eyes, and I felt as if I was sitting before a ghost.

"I am Sana," I said softly, "your brother's daughter." I waited for a response as I observed him slowly turn to his side a little. I could see his shoulder blades protruding out from underneath his shirt.

His expression suddenly changed. "Why have you come?" he said, his voice weak and barely audible.

"Wouldn't you want to know what kind of life I have had? You know that my father was killed in cold blood. My mother had to remarry, I was separated from my family, and my life was ruined. But there is one thing you do not know: I know who killed my papa. I was there to witness his murder. I was nine years old. I was hiding behind the curtain and I saw your face right after you had killed him. I saw him die before my eyes and I have had to live with that every single day of my life. I remembered your face. I promised never to forget you for as long as I lived."

He tried to sit up but was too frail for the endeavor. The sunlight shifted and the room became less dark. I could see his face more clearly and I noticed that his skin was pale, with a tinge of yellow. The white of his eyes also appeared yellow. I was beginning to wonder if he had hepatitis.

He reached over to have a sip of water from a silver metallic bowl, or *katora,* which sat at his bedside, "Why did it take you so many years to come here? I wish you had come sooner. I wish you had come that same night."

This was not the meeting I had anticipated. This was not the man I had been waiting to confront. And this was certainly not the reaction I had predicted.

"Because I was naïve," I said. "I was a child and believed whatever I was told. I was informed that the killer had been caught and was serving a life sentence. I assumed it was you. I could never have imagined that an innocent person was suffering behind the walls of prison. When I went to meet him, I knew they had the wrong man. How could you ruin our lives and then let an innocent person be punished for your crime? How do you sleep at night?"

My face felt warm with anger, but I also felt some sense of peace that I was not in danger and that I had been able to say many of the things I had planned to say for years. My enemy was still my enemy but he appeared helpless and unable to cause harm in his current debilitated state. I suddenly felt safe and confident.

"When I saw your picture in my family album, I could not believe that the person who took my father's life was his own brother. I love my brother so much that I would give my life for him, even though we haven't lived in the same house for most of our lives. And you killed your own brother in cold blood. If you would have asked, just asked one time, for money or land, he would have given it to you in a heartbeat. He didn't care for things. He cared about people, about family, and about life. So now that you have all those things, are you happy? Are you happy that my father's dead and an innocent man's sixteen years have been thrown away? Did you think about the fact that these two people have families? How could you take our lives away?"

After a pause he responded, "I didn't know. I didn't know that someone else was in prison. What I did was horrible, unforgivable. And I don't expect you to forgive me at all. You can kill me if you wish. But I do want to tell you some things if you would care to listen. It may give you some comfort."

"I am listening," I said, still seething with rage.

"It had nothing to do with money. I was ten years old when my father—your grandfather—left us. We had a glorious life until then, a life full of happiness and laughter. Abba loved my mother and me to death, or so it seemed. He taught me math, he told me stories, and he stayed up all night with me when I had a fever. He taught me how to play cricket and how to ride a horse. He was the best father, and we were the perfect family. But one day he suddenly left us. He was gone from our home and from our lives. He had found another woman with whom he wanted to spend the rest of his life. She was more educated than my mother, and he felt that they would have a better understanding. I heard him say those hurtful words so casually, as if he were simply uttering a weather update. I heard my mother cry and scream all night and beg my father not to leave us. She said she would live with the other woman. We could all live together and make adjustments. But my father said the other woman was not agreeable to that arrangement.

"My mother changed overnight. She changed from a loving, caring wife and mother to a living corpse. She eventually lost her mind and had to be institutionalized. He said he would continue to visit us and support us financially; he was a 'gentleman' after all. Gradually the visits became more infrequent and then stopped altogether. The financial support continued, however."

He paused to cough and to regain the strength that had been consumed by conversing. "I had been a good student; I always stood ahead of my classmates, mainly because I had an educated father, unlike most children in the village. But when he left, I became a lost, abandoned child. All my desire to succeed vanished. Who would I need to make proud? My mother who barely recognized me, or my father who couldn't care less? The only wish I had was to sever ties with my father so that we were not dependent on him for money. I started working in my teenage years to support the needs of my mother and refused to take a single rupee from him. Did he think that money could buy us happiness? That it could cover the scars he had left inside us? I became more depressed when I learned of your father's birth and then your aunt's arrival. They were the happy family now, the family built on the ruins of our broken home.

"I let hatred grow inside me until it became so strong that it was like a volcano. Over time, your father became everything I had wanted to become and more. He received the best education and the best guidance from my father. He did not miss a day of his affection. He never knew what it was like to have your life taken away from you like that. I could have had the same opportunities had I allowed my father to be part of my life. For several years, I was consumed by the hard labor on the farm and factories. I had to work extra shifts to pay the expenses of the facility that housed my psychotic mother. After she passed away, I got married and had a son. I spent so much time and energy hating your father that I neglected my own family. I had promised to always be there for them, unlike my father, but I was so determined to hate and avenge that I failed to fulfill my promise.

"Many years went by. One day I was looking at old photographs of my father and me, and my son, Taimur, who was seven at the time, began asking me questions about him that I could not answer. Finally the volcano erupted. I had a gun, which I loaded, and set off to kill my own brother. This would be the ultimate revenge, the most severe punishment for my father, even though he had long been in his grave. I was sure I would get caught, given the high security and the social importance your father enjoyed. I thought I would be put to death and that would end my misery. I did not think at that instant of his family, his wife, and his two beautiful children, nor did I think of what my actions would do to my own family. I had completely lost my senses. Not a moment goes by that I don't regret what I did or that I didn't get caught. What happened to me was far worse than that. That is why I want you to hear the rest of my story."

He turned a bit, clutched his abdomen in some pain, coughed weakly in an attempt to clear his throat, and resumed. "I saw your father sitting in his study, and the broken window between us. As soon as I let the bullets escape, I felt the shame of what I had done. I grabbed the watch and the wallet, because they were within my reach. My impulse was to take them so it would seem like a robbery. But as soon as I saw him lying there, I regretted my actions. I felt as if I had died. Shame and guilt are horrible things; they can eat you up inside until there is nothing left. I stopped for a moment and then I ran. What I did was unforgivable. I don't expect you or God or anyone to forgive me. But it never was about money; it was about my father's love. I ran because I wanted to run far away from myself; I wanted to run into another world where all this wasn't reality but a horrid dream. Surely they would find me, I thought, and justice would be served to some degree. It never occurred to me that they hadn't come searching for me because they had already put someone else in prison. I came home a changed man.

"It is said that justice is always served—if not in this life, then in the hereafter. But I was punished. Not in the traditional sense of being put in prison, but in a worse way. I was tormented the whole night, unable to sleep, and at about six o'clock the next morning, I had finally closed my eyes for a brief moment when I heard a loud bang that was as loud as the bullets I had fired the night before. In the trance that I had been in, I had left my loaded gun sitting on the chair. Taimur had thought that it was a toy gun I had brought him as a present from the city, and had accidentally shot himself. My son bled to death before my eyes, and there was nothing I could do to save him. It was as if I had killed him myself."

He paused to wipe his tears before continuing, "After burying him, I came home a nearly insane man. I wish I had gone completely insane like my mother so I wouldn't feel the pain. But the pain remained, and to this day I feel it deep and fresh, like it just happened a moment ago. My wife could never come to terms with the loss, and after a few months, she left me. I live with what I have done every minute of my life. I have been punished for it. I now have pancreatic cancer, and the pain is so unbearable, it's like a gnawing bullet in the pit of my stomach. But this bullet does not kill so easily. It is a slow, painful death."

"By the time the diagnosis was made, it was already too late; it had spread to my liver and lungs. I did not want chemotherapy or even the treatments to alleviate my pain. I wanted to suffer and I wanted to die. I wanted to pay for my sins. I had promised to be a better father to my son than my father had been to me. My father had only left his son, but I had killed my son; he was dead because of me. I had a loving wife and a wonderful son who could have helped me forget my past and build a new life, but instead I let my hatred ruin it all. Now I have no one. The lady who opened the door is a maid. She is here because she gets paid to make my meals. Death is near, Sana, and there is no one even to bury me."

He looked up, and I saw that the glassy look in his eyes had been replaced by an earnest plea of mercy from a dying man.

Chapter 18

I felt a new kind of sadness overcome me. The anger, the hatred, and the desire for revenge had suddenly shrunk. For years I had desperately wanted my father's killer to suffer and to feel the pain my father had felt when he had lost his life. But at that moment, I felt pity for the dying man lying helpless before me.

It was a relief to me that my father's death had not been about money or about things, because it had always bothered me that my father had lost his life to such trivial matters. It had not been about material possessions at all; it had been about love. It had been about a father's love that was snatched away—a cord cut suddenly and brutally—an emotion that no one understood better than I did. He had let hatred and resentment become the center of his life, as I had, and his anger had destroyed him.

Soon another thought entered my fatigued mind. Had I spoken the truth right away, the police might have caught him and taken possession of his gun, and perhaps the little innocent Taimur's life could have been spared. I wondered if the responsibility of his accidental death also rested on my shoulders. Could I carry such a heavy burden for the rest of my life? If he was dead because of me, this had not been the revenge I had desired. It was the ultimate revenge, the ultimate punishment for my worst enemy, yet it did not appease me to see this man's pain or hear the narration of his unthinkable, incomparable loss.

Slowly, hesitantly, I held out my hand to my uncle and said, "I am so sorry for your loss."

I could never have predicted the words I was saying to my father's assassin. "I can never forget the pain of my father's loss and I will never be able to justify your actions. I miss him every single day. When you were missing your father, I wish you had considered that the person you were killing was a father as well. But in order to move ahead with my life, I must forgive you. And even though I had wanted the worst for you, it breaks my heart to hear about your boy. And you are not alone."

He looked up at me, his green eyes full of sadness and defeat, albeit a different one from the one I had seen in Ahmer's father's eyes. This was a greater defeat: that of a life lost, but also of a spirit lost.

"You have a very big heart, like your father's," he said. "I know why death had not yet come to me; it was because I needed to hear your forgiving words in order to have some peace before I die."

The weapon to heal my sorrow was in my hands at last.

"I just need you to do something for me." I said.

"Anything," he replied.

"I need you to give a statement of confession to the police so that an innocent man can be exonerated. He has suffered enough."

My uncle was unable to travel, so I arranged for an officer to go over to record his confession. His possession of the watch gave further credence to his story.

When I delved deeper, I discovered that Ahmer's father had actually met Papa on the dreaded day. He had wished to inquire about the process of taking his wife to America for her cancer treatment, and a common friend had referred him to Papa, who knew well the details of obtaining visas for medical reasons. Since he had been the last person to meet my father outside the family and his fingerprints were on the paperwork that Papa had taken home, he had been an easy target for a forced confession. It had been a high-profile murder, and the police department had been determined to show that they had caught and punished the killer. The designated lead investigator's promotion had depended on it.

In a matter of days, Ahmer's father was released from prison. I watched from my car, which was hidden behind the bushes so no one could see me. I needed to witness this magical moment, even if I could not participate in it. Ahmer walked toward the black iron gate, eager and expectant, and his father walked away from it, dressed in civilian clothes—a white-collared shirt and a pair of striped brown trousers. He walked with his head held high, leaving behind the walls that had punished him, harassed him, confined him, and disgraced him for sixteen long years. His gait was like that of a child who had just learned to walk; reluctant, yet simultaneously unstoppable in his newly discovered world. He was clean-shaven, with the dimple in his chin now clearly visible and his gray hair evenly trimmed and meticulously combed. It was as though he had prepared himself to confront the new Universe. Despite all the lines that years of anguish had ruthlessly drawn on his face, a glimpse of youth emanated from his being. From a distance I could make out his eyes as he squinted and turned away slightly from the brightness of the blazing sun. He inhaled deeply the fresh air, not noticing the smoke and dust that clung to it, gracefully welcoming all aspects of his new found freedom.

Father and son hugged one another for several minutes, holding on tightly and allowing tears that had accumulated for a decade and a half to fall to the ground. They did not place their palms on their faces to halt them or use a tissue to dry them. They did not pretend that the wind had blown sand into their eyes. Ahmer looked at the gate with one final, accusatory, unforgiving look, but his father did not turn to look back. He looked only at his grown son standing before him, his eyes filled to the brim with the utmost gratitude for this reunion. It was the profound moment when Ahmer found an expanse of peace and I a morsel of atonement.

The court had decided not to pursue punishment for my uncle in light of the fact that his oncologist had given him a life expectancy of less than a month. He passed peacefully at his home the day following the release, as if he had indeed been holding on to his last breath to meet me. What if he had died before I had been able to discover his identity? Then I would have never had the chance to bring closure to my lifelong ordeal, and Ahmer's father would never have been a free man. I had been reckless in my procrastination, but God had been kind. He had been kind to a girl who had needed to know the truth. He had led me to Ahmer, and through him, I had learned of everything that had been hidden from me. The dream I had had about Ahmer, with him taking me on horseback toward a bright rising sun, had materialized. He had helped me overcome my fear and anger and had led me to the light, which had symbolized the truth. In the process, however, I had lost Ahmer himself. But while I had lost my love, I had won something much greater than the fulfillment of my own dreams.

I had called Phuppo and convinced her to plan a trip because I really needed to meet her. My mother, brother, and aunt had been in the dark until the day of the confession, when I finally called them and asked that we all meet. I told them that I had something very important to share with them. They expected it would be something about my broken engagement and definitely had not expected something as consequential as the truth I was about to disclose. They all believed that my father's assassination was buried in the past. By now my brother was far older than I had been at the time of my father's death, and I was sure that letting him in on this secret would no longer be considered a betrayal of the promise I had made to my mother. I also believed it was important for him to hear the truth, so he could understand me better. Maybe now he could answer the question he had asked me many times before: Apa why did you leave? He needed to know what secret I had carried with me as a child and how heavy the burden of that secret had been on my young shoulders.

My mother was shocked to hear everything. On the night of the murder, she had been so overwhelmed with grief that she had not realized that I had witnessed the shooting or that I had been there before her. She had been too distraught to appear in court for the arraignment. And later she had been so wrapped up in her new family, putting every morsel of her being into making her second marriage work, that she had never questioned the authenticity of the investigation surrounding my father's killing. She reassured me that I was not at all to blame for the chain of tragedies that followed. I was a child, after all, and she was the adult. I was a child, after all, and a traumatized one at that, and she was the adult.

Several days later, Sahir said, "Apa, even if Ammi forbade you to tell me something, you should have shared it with me, if not immediately then maybe a few years later. You are the one who always told me that sorrow is halved when it's shared, just as happiness is doubled. How could you keep all this inside you for so long? And I might have never known if it hadn't been for all these coincidences that brought everything together."

"I thought I would tell you when you grew older, but when you did, I thought it might disturb the normalcy you had found in your new life and your new family. Plus the only positive thing I had given Ammi was the promise I made and honored, and I did not wish to lose that."

"Did you think I didn't know how Papa died? When I was eight, a bunch of kids at school were talking about it. I beat them up then, not believing it, but then when I heard the same story from other people a year later, I realized it was true. I wasn't sure that you knew, that's why I didn't dare ask you. I just buried myself in my books, so I could push everything else away. Many years later, I looked it up on the internet."

Suddenly I realized that both of us had been alone in our suffering. I said, "I am sad that you did not grow up without pain, as I had hoped. I wish you would have told me that you knew. I wish I had said something. I had started to think of myself as an outsider. You had another, better sister; I felt that Sara had replaced me."

"Come on, Apa, what are you saying? There can never be a replacement of you. Sara is my younger sister, and I love her to death. I tease her and I take care of her. But you are my big sister and you are the *only* big sister. I was very young when Papa died, but I remember how you took care of me then. Even Ammi could not give me the comfort your words gave me. If I ever have a problem, you are the one I go to for advice; you are my confidante. That's why I feel let down that you did not tell me such a big thing. But I am so very proud of you for what you have done. You have brought justice in a country where the very term 'justice' is a word of mockery now."

My mother gave me a hug that was both warm and all-embracing. It was the hug I had craved when my father had died. "You are so brave," she said. "You got that from your father. I was never brave. I was always weak—a conformer. That was the only reason I married so soon after your father's death."

From the corner of my eye I could see her eyes fill up with tears and her lashes flicker with remembrance of days past. "One thing I didn't tell you then was that your grandfather had known he was dying. His cardiologist had told him that his heart was functioning poorly and that he did not have much time. I didn't want to tell you because you had already faced so many shocks. But I was really scared; I had just lost my husband and knew I would soon lose my father. He was worried for me and made me promise him that I would marry so he could be assured that someone would take care of me, you, and Sahir after his demise. I agreed at the time, but I have regretted that decision, not because your stepfather is not a nice man, but because it took you away from me. I am a wife, but before that I was—and am and should have been—a mother. I have never been able to forgive myself for that. I should have asked you, and if you were not ready, I should have let it go, even if that meant never having a second chance. And there can never, ever be a replacement of you. You are my special daughter. You are the one who carried all the burden of tragedy on your shoulders and took care of everything all by yourself."

"But I should have listened to Papa's last words," I said. "I should have kept that pearl of wisdom in a shell and treasured it, rather than letting it fall into a river of tears. I shouldn't have hidden the truth. So much sorrow has come from that."

"Don't look back, dear. Look ahead. If it weren't for you, an innocent man would have spent his entire life in prison. He would have died there, Sana. And now he may live another fifty years; who knows?"

"But his son will never forgive me, Ammi. His father suffered such humiliation. He was separated from his family and had his freedom taken away. Do you know his vision is poor because he has not looked into the distance for years and his eyes cannot focus on objects that are far? Many of the years he was incarcerated he was in chains, so it's hard for him to walk. Once a fellow prisoner beat him up so badly that his tooth broke. He didn't have anyone visit him in prison, because many of his friends and relatives believed he might be guilty, so they cut off all ties with him. His only visitor was Ahmer, who was at the other end of the world and could not visit him more than once a year. There have been countless changes in the universe around him, but he is frozen in time and space. I can never give him back all the time he has lost. His son will never forgive me."

All the tears I had held back started pouring like a waterfall, soaking my hands. These were tears of loss. I had spent half my life grieving for my father and would probably spend the other half grieving for the love I had lost. What a glorious, happily married life I could have had. Soon the memories of the wonderful times we had spent together—the path we had walked, the conversations we had shared, the life we had dreamed of—would all start to blur, like a picture gradually going out of focus. But I would not be able to preserve those precious moments or relive those timeless memories in my mind as I had archived and unapologetically cherished the memories of my father. I would have to let them die or be buried in a part of my mind where even I myself could never retrieve them. What I had thought to be imprints on stone, were in actuality footprints on sand, waiting to be washed gently away. I would marry Zain and try my best to be a devoted wife and caring mother. I would never see Ahmer again and would let his memory leave me like the fading fragrance of a dying flower. I thought of how I had cried in that scene of *Devdas* where the girl was in love with Devdas but was tying the matrimonial knot with another man. The scene of her saying goodbye to him played before me like a vivid flashback. I did not know how I would go through with it. But I had gone through with a lot of things, had I not?

"He will never forgive me," I repeated, grabbing hold of a tissue.

My mother put her arm around me. "He has already forgiven you, Sana."

Chapter 19

I looked up, surprised. "You know Ahmer?" I asked, bewildered.

"He was here this morning with his father and asked for your hand in marriage. He is a wonderful boy. In my heart I said yes, but I told him I would need to ask you first. I know it's complicated having our families unite in this way after all that has passed between us. But as long as both of you can get past it, we all want to make it happen. Ahmer's father is a generous soul, and I did not see anger in his eyes or hear resentment in his voice. After all that you have both gone through, you deserve nothing but sheer happiness."

I could not believe that this was truly happening. Ahmer and I had not spoken since I had turned down his marriage proposal. The last time I had seen him was when I had blatantly said good-bye when he had been taking me to meet his father. I had gone back a second and then a third time to visit his father so I could explain everything. I told him about the reason for my abrupt departure and my role in ruining his life. I cried inconsolably, but he reassured me, and I saw tears of happiness fill his eyes. He wore an expression not of hatred but of gratitude. He did not see me as an end to his past life, but rather a beginning to a new one. I was his ray of hope, his light at the end of this very long, dark tunnel. I was his usher to the new, changing outside world. I was the sunshine that would light up a lifetime of darkness. I was the bridge that would reunite him with his son. He was a generous man, giving me credit for his freedom rather than blame for his confinement. He saw me as his key out of prison, not as the handcuffs that had locked him away. What a big heart he had to be able to overlook every minute of every day that he had spent unfairly in a cell smaller than a washroom, where he had inhaled toxic fumes and washed his face with muddy waters, had felt the sting of injustice and the stab of humiliation, and had lost in seconds the respect it had taken him decades to earn.

"I had always been an optimist, even after what happened to me, but over the last few years, I had really started losing hope of ever being a free man, walking to my son with my head held high," he had said. "Now I will be able to do it."

"I should have come earlier. Sorry is such a small word for the amount of pain I have inflicted on you and your family. I cannot adequately convey what I feel."

"Don't be sorry, Sana. You have saved me. I will not die here. I will not die a death of dishonor. I may have years ahead of me, and once you have spent time in this place, every single day becomes so much more valuable. I have so much to do. I had promised myself and God that if I ever got out of here, I would get involved in something meaningful, such as prison reform. There is so much to do. There are so many breaths of fresh air to take and so many good days ahead of me. I am so proud of my son for choosing you to spend the rest of his life with. Now I want to come home not only to my son but also to my daughter."

Even after his father's words of salvation, Ahmer continued to be angry with me, and I could not blame him. Following his father's release, he had tried to contact me again, but I did not answer. I was not sure if he wished to talk to me to unleash his anger or simply to remind me of all the ways in which I had destroyed his life.

I was dumbfounded that he had come to my home with a marriage proposal. I still did not think I deserved his affection but I agreed to meet him. When we sat down to talk, he said, "I was angry with you, Sana, but not because I blamed you for anything. My falling in love with you was a strange coincidence, but that's what eventually led to my father's freedom. Something I had prayed for day after day and night after night I got because of you. Over the years, my quest for freeing my father had become full of setbacks and dashed hopes. Many times it seemed like a fruitless endeavor. I just wanted to give it everything I had in me and fight the case myself, but that seemed full of difficulties. The red tape, the lack of good documentation, the corrupt police system: these were all things I was only beginning to understand. A master's degree in international law from Stanford cannot stand up against all the problems within our judicial system.

"I was angry because you left without saying a word. For me, there is nothing that can come between us—ever. If you build a bridge, I will burn it. If you make an iceberg, I will melt it. When you left, it seemed as though you had left for good. I didn't think you'd ever return to hear my side of the story. I had always known that my dad was innocent, and I knew I would be able to convince you of that, if only you would have given me the chance. After all I had convinced you of so many other things in the past, helping you see the other side. I couldn't believe you were ready to throw it all away, all that we had."

"I am sorry, Ahmer. I was so overwhelmed, I didn't know what to say or do. I just had to get away. When I discovered the truth, the tables turned, and I was simply too ashamed to face you. I needed to sort everything out before I could look into your eyes again."

He paused for a few seconds before saying, "So are you ready to look into my eyes every day of your life?"

I met his gaze and saw a sparkle in his eyes; this time, he knew what my answer was going to be. "Yes, Ahmer. I want to spend my life with you. It is because of you that I have love and peace and honor in my life. I knew you were the one when I first met you. I was sure the day you gave me your umbrella that, I could face all the storms in my life if you were by my side. You are a giving, kind soul. You inspire me to write. You make me want to be a better person. You make me want to live."

"Do you really think I would have given you up to Zain?"

"No. I was thinking of saying yes to him just as a punishment for myself. I wanted to force myself to forget you."

"And would you have been able to?"

"No."

"That would have been unfair to everybody, would it not? And I have higher expectations from you, Sana. You wouldn't do something that reckless. And if you tried, I would fight for you till I won. You know how persistent I can be. I am not Devdas, you know."

"I want you to have something," I said, bringing him my father's silver watch, which my uncle had given back to me. It was accompanied with a card that read,

"I pray that the times will be kind to us."

Shortly after, we were married. It was a simple, elegant wedding, just as both of us had envisioned, with a nontraditionally brief guest list. I did not want to be one of those people who spent all the time preparing for the wedding rather than preparing for the marriage. I do not know whether I looked beautiful, but I do know that I felt beautiful inside.

Ammi put her arms around Phuppo and said to her, "I was torn to pieces when she left me. I was angry with you for years because you supported her. But now I know that what began as a rebellious moment, resulted in a beautiful daughter for all of us. I am indebted to you for raising her so well. I couldn't have done a better job."

Not a moment passed that I did not think of my father. I pictured how he might have looked, his hair a full salt and pepper, some early wrinkles setting in at the edges of his smile. I wondered if he would have liked Ahmer and thought about how much he would have missed me after I left his nest. When I thought of him now, I thought about his love and his wisdom, which I hoped he had passed down to me and which one day I would, God willing, pass down to my children. I could love him without hating someone else. I could cherish his memories without being angry and bitter. I could now look at his life and what it had given me rather than dwelling on the single moment of his painful death and what it had taken away.

Epilogue

May 2011: Pakistan was led for several years by General Pervaiz Musharraf, who was seen by many as a ray of hope but by many, including the western world, as a dictator. We witnessed some economic progress, a leap towards modernization. News media flourished under his reign, like a bird that had been freed from its cage. There was a steady increase in accountability and a parallel decline in corruption.

My son, Arsal, was born in 2007, which was a magical, miraculous time that brought me the most intoxicating joy I had ever known. Later that year, on December 27, Pakistan witnessed yet another assassination—that of Benazir Bhutto. Pervaiz Musharraf stepped down as president, and Benazir's husband, Asif Ali Zardari, was elected president shortly after the tragedy. Pervaiz Musharraf had not only improved things in Pakistan in general terms but had played a crucial role in stabilizing Pakistan's economy and was seen by the West as an important ally in the war against terror. However poor judgment in opposing the judiciary had led to his downfall and forced resignation. Pakistan's fate seemed precarious once again.

After much deliberation, we decided to settle down in Pakistan. I know I will always have a home in America, and I try to go every other year, for my aunt and uncle continue to be an integral part of my life. Some years ago, we went to New York and visited Ground Zero. It was touching to see the silhouettes of the victims, their list of names, and the heartfelt tributes families and friends had paid. It was a perfect portrayal of my sentiments that every person counts and every life matters. I spent some time in silence, gazing at the pictures, reading each name, and thinking about how close Ahmer had come to having his name on that tragic list. I wondered how my life would have turned out had Ahmer taken Flight 93. I would probably have never married or had any children, or I would have spent decades being part of a loveless marriage to Zain. Worse still, Ahmer's father might still have been in jail and would have died there mourning the loss of his only son, who had promised to get him out. In 2005 too, I travelled to San Francisco to stay with my aunt and meet up with Jennifer. I was able to attend the graduation ceremony at Stanford that year as part of the alumni association. Steve Jobs had given a memorable commencement speech as we fanned ourselves with the program schedule to ward off the heat.

"You can only connect the dots looking back, not looking forward. So you should hope that your dots will somehow connect in your future," he had said. He had encouraged the graduating class to live their own dreams and never settle.

In Pakistan, I am trying to live my dream. I joined the national news channel, Geo, which means "to live." Earlier this year, I participated in preparing a documentary about Faiz Ahmed Faiz in honor of his hundredth birthday. His words, written long ago, are still relevant today:

When will a pure, unblemished spring come into view?
After how many rainfalls will the bloodstains be washed away?

Faiz's daughter said that he did not write simply about despair or gloom; there was hope in his words, but one had to search for it, as one has to search for it in every aspect of life.

A few weeks ago, when I had stopped thinking of Osama bin Laden and had started believing that he was either dead or would never be found, we got word in the newsroom that he had been captured and killed in Abbotabad in Pakistan. The day the news came, Arsal asked me, "Who is bin Laden, Mummy?"

It was a complicated question that no parenting book had prepared me to answer. "Maybe you can ask Papa," was my hesitant reply. At his age he would not be able to comprehend such evil, the distortion and abuse of religion, the international struggles for power, or the ironic retrogression of the civilized world. Osama had been captured nowhere near the Pakistan-Afghanistan border, the targeted area for the drone strikes. It was unclear what Pakistan's involvement had been in the capture, but it was perplexing that the most wanted man in the world had been hiding in our country for six years. I hope but doubt that bin Laden's death will bring an end to al-Qaeda. I pray that there will be no other date as dreaded as 9/11 for America. I pray that there will be no more drone strikes that kill innocent civilians in the comfort of their modest homes in Pakistan.

More than thirty-five thousand people have been killed in Pakistan in the aftermath of 9/11, their deaths the result of a combination of suicide bombings and target killings. That list includes thirty-four journalists. Unfortunately this has become such an everyday occurrence that people have become numb to the pain of it. There is no monument dedicated to those who perished at the hands of terrorism in Pakistan. I hope that one day my son can be proud of a Pakistan that is free of poverty, of hunger, and of the corrupt leadership that has contaminated this country. I pray that there will be no child who is misled and taught the table of hatred and misconstrued religious values, no child who is deprived of a childhood and thrown into the world of suicide bombing. I pray that our country will one day be free of the discrepancies between rich and poor and the divide between religious extremists and the overly modern. I pray for a day when, as Fatima Bhutto said, there will be enough refrigerators to house polio vaccines in a country that is a nuclear state. I pray that the literacy rate will not be amongst the lowest in a country estimated to be among the top five nations on the global intelligence scale. I hope that the leaders of the world will remember the reason that the United Nations was created and that wars both official and unofficial will become a thing of the past. I hope that my city can overcome this darkness and once again become the City of Lights. I hope that my country can one day live up to its name, Land of the Pure.

The people of Pakistan all came together in the earthquake of 2005 and the floods of 2010, which killed thousands of people and rendered many more homeless. Volunteers generously offered their money, their belongings, their prayers, and their time. These good citizens made the relief efforts successful amidst the chaos created by the state of lawlessness.

Today I am going to pick four-year-old Arsal up from school. He looks like both Ahmer and me. It is heartwarming to see what a good father Ahmer is. Arsal does not have my dad, but he does have three grandfathers who love to spoil him: My Uncle, Ahmer's father, who I call Baba, and my stepfather, with whom I have reestablished a new bond through my son and who I now call Abbu. Sara is getting married in a few months, and the wedding preparations are in full swing. She comes over often to visit me but mostly to play with Arsal, who is the apple of her eye. Sahir's grueling surgery residency is nearing completion, and I pray that he will catch up on some of his years of sleepless nights. He is married to Maryam, and they are expecting their first child. It is ironic that he has been in America all this time since I moved back to Pakistan. Despite the physical distance, our bond is stronger than ever before. Ahmer's aunt visits often; she is now cancer free.

I roll down the window to let my hair bathe in the Karachi breeze. It is a hot day but is cooler than what is typical for this time of year. The smoke from the buses and the noise of the continuous honking of the horns no longer bothers me. I can hear the *koyal* as she sings softly her announcement that the mangoes are ripe and ready to be eaten. I feel like a replanted tree once again, yet my bond with my family as well as my country feels stronger, and the love feels more reciprocated. I turn on the radio, and the Strings song "*Mein tho dekhoon Ga*" is playing; it has lately become Arsal's favorite. I sing along:

I will see, I will see,
And you will see as well,
When bread will be cheap and life will be priceless,
That day will come again,
That's how Pakistan will be
I will see, I will see,
You will see
When children will reign over the country

I check my phone and see that Kavita has replied to my e-mail; she will be able to make it for Sara's wedding. We have not met for years, though she lives nearby, in India. I am so pleased that I will finally see her children in real life rather than simply witnessing their escapades on Face book. Jennifer is good at keeping in touch, and her blonde jokes continue to entertain us. Ahmer is a practicing lawyer, and other than his long hours, I seldom have complaints. He works as a defense lawyer and has helped reopen many cold cases and exonerate countless innocent prisoners. We both work closely with his father, who has now established an NGO for prisoners. Zareen's eldest daughter, Ayesha, has recently passed her matriculation exams and is soon to embark on a college education. She will be the first girl—and possibly the first person in her family—to complete all ten grades. Zareen cannot change the past but she is living her dream through the achievements of her children.

A bracelet with a dozen pearls adorns my wrist, and I tell Arsal that each pearl is for every valuable lesson I have learned in my life. He always asks me what he should do with the lessons he learns, since boys do not wear bracelets, and I tell him, "You can carry them in your heart; that way you will protect them and never lose them, like I once did long ago."

Despite the insecurities and the everyday tragedies around us, life goes on. I try to make the world around Arsal as beautiful as every child's world should be. Some days ago, we went to Jimmy's Studio to have a family portrait taken. We were having difficulty deciding whether Arsal should wear the red or the striped blue shirt and whether the background should be beige or black. Finally we chose the red shirt and the beige background, and the photographer was able to capture Arsal with the most radiant smile. On the way to school, I picked up the enlargement and a bronze frame to go with it. I must say, it turned out just perfect.

Acknowledgements

I am indebted to my husband Omer Zuberi for patiently listening to the narration of my book and encouraging me as I toiled; my parents Surriya and Babar Zuberi for passing on to me their love of books, as well as offering their valuable insight at every stage of the manuscript; Nasima Zuberi, Manzar Zuberi and Sweta Gandhi for their keen eyes and sound editing advice. I am grateful to my publishing consultant, Stephanie Robinson, who guided me through the publishing process. I thank all those who read the novel in its infancy and believed in it: Fadieleh Aidrus, Faiza Saadaat, Muzna Shamsi, Naasha Talati, Rehana Kundawala, Shahida Bashir and my youngest reader, Samad Khalid. I also want to thank my friend Sunita Khetpal for reminding me of my long forgotten childhood dream of writing a novel, and the Createspace team for making it a reality.

Lara Zuberi was brought up in Pakistan, and now lives in Jacksonville, Florida with her husband and son. This is her debut novel.

Made in the USA
Charleston, SC
18 February 2013